when the ice breaks

KJ Sosa

for all of the people who kept going when grief tried to tear them apart.

for mamma,
Thank you for believing in me. I love you.

for toby,
Thanks for always being there for me. Payton wouldn't be here
without you. Love you man.

preface

While yes, this is a book meant for teens, this is still a story that deals with heavier topics of mental health. I hope that I can say that I handled these topics well with sensitivity and care. There are still many parts that can be a bit heavy and could possibly be difficult to read. If any of these become too much for you to handle, or you don't feel like you'll be able to handle it, it may be best for you to leave this book be. Your mental health matters more, I promise. <3

Graphic: Mentions of Death/Death of a Parent, Guilt, Grief, Severe Anxiety

Moderate: Destructive Behavior/Self-Harm, Depression/Low Self-worth,

Mild: Discussions of Identity

end of summer

The Beginning

prologue

The walk back home after work is always my favorite part of the day. I get to listen to my music and block out everything while I count the grooves between the sidewalk panels. Doesn't help much that my mom spams my phone whenever I'm out later than when work is over.

Like right now.

I stayed late for a little extra cash and forgot to tell her.

Don't get me wrong, I know why she does it, but she doesn't even give me a chance to text back. Once I start typing, I get a new message. I think she sets some kinda record for how fast she types. As soon as I'm about to hit send, she calls me.

Of course.

When I answer, I'm pretty sure she can be heard shouting through my earbuds.

"Payton, where on Earth are you! You said you'd be back at 10:30, it's 11!" she exclaims, as I unplug my phone and hold it up to my ear.

"I got out late—no that's not—stuff just happens, I for—Mom. Mom!"

That's really all I can get out as she keeps going.

"It's like you forget what happened last time! Are you trying to give me a heart attack?" she half-laughs through the speaker but I can hear her pushing down the fear in her voice.

I hate when she brings this up.

Like, she shouldn't get to throw my trauma back into my face. Yeah, sure, it's hers too, but she wasn't there. She doesn't know what it was like.

I'm never sure how to respond either. I rub my hand on my neck, lightly going over a scar, sighing.

By the time I finally come up with something to say, two people come out of nowhere, laughing softly as they leave the bistro.

Everything happens so fast, and the next thing I know I'm dropping my phone and covered in hot tea, pulling back like I am retracing my steps.

"Oh my god- I'm so sorry!" one of them squeaks. "I didn't see you!"

I'm just trying to find my phone, please, this is embarrassing. "It's fine," I say quickly, before actually looking up at her.

They're still talking but I don't process anything they're saying, I just see their eyes. Greener than grass. They're pretty. They're horrified, that much I can tell. But, there's something else there. I don't know.

I look down again—I just need to get my phone and go.

Just as I spot it near the now empty cup, we both bend down to grab it

"Sorry—" they laugh, then flash a small but shy sweet smile.

I don't really know what to say again, so I just return the smile and pick up my phone.

"Uhm—have a good night—" I manage to get out before speed-walking away.

I hear them call out to me but I just want to be done with this horrific interaction. I'm not good at people. Out of the corner of my ear, I still hear something. I assume I'm far enough away, so I check my phone.

Mom. *Shit.*

"Mom—Mom! I'm sorry. No, I'm fine. It's just— Mom. Bad connection." I sigh, putting the phone to my ear. "I'm on my way right now, ok?"

I'm not ready for the rant she's definitely going to give me later.

quarter 1

"I've found that with depression, it's not that I don't want to get better, it's that I don't know how." - Kate Hudson

chapter one

No matter how many times we do this it's always a fight. Every time she asks, I say no. It's like a dance, but every time it ends, we start right back up again. I love my mom, but she never knows when to quit.

"But listen, I've been looking," she says, pulling my computer towards her as she sits next to me. "And I found this place while I was at work."

She turns my computer back towards us revealing a bright blue and pastel yellow page with **The Vermont Resilience Institute** written in a pastel baby blue. Underneath it read:

Nurture your mind, Nurture your life, with an evaluation form link attached to the tagline.

"I don't need this. How many times do I have to tell you I'm fine," I say, trying to brush her off.

I fail.

"Oh really?"

"Yes."

"Then what did I hear last night?" she asks. "I specifically recall hearing someone leave his room at nearly 2:00 A.M."

"What, I can't use the bathroom anymore?"

"I heard you. I know your nightmares are back," she finally says.

How do you even respond to that? I watch her study me. She may be a midwife but her second degree in psychology is enough to ruin any reality of me keeping things to myself. She's good at reading people, at least on a surface level. But if she were better at it on a deeper scale, I'd be screwed.

"Just look into it." She pats my back. "For me."

"Fine... but I promise nothing." I huff.

She stands from her chair and plants a kiss on my forehead before moving towards her purse.

"That's all I ask." She smiles.

"I have a few errands to run later and then I have a night shift." She rummages through her purse, finally pulling out a smaller makeup bag and the car keys. "You'll be alright tonight?" she asks, removing the cap from her tube of lipstick.

Light pink was always a good color on her. At least my dad always used to say so. I think he was right. It brings out her eyes, really makes her other features pop. My mom is pretty, I think in every form of the word. Even her name is pretty. Isabella. But she doesn't wear pink much anymore. She's got her lipstick and that's all. It's the shade my dad bought her on their first wedding anniversary, no wonder she holds onto it.

"Nothing I can't handle. Is Ashleigh coming over?" I ask.

"Only if you call her. She's seventeen, she has a life." She laughs. "But I'm sure Millie isn't that much of a hassle."

Four month olds are more than just a "hassle", but okay. "When do you need us home? I know Austin wanted to go to the Beanstalk."

"My shift starts at six so...I'd say between five to five-thirty?"

I nod, looking over to my computer and switching tabs to see the syllabus for my physics class. Job applications can wait, the thought of three jobs is nerve-wracking enough.

I watch mom go into her bedroom empty handed and come back out with my baby sister in her arms. "*We* will be back later," she says, holding Millie's hand up to wave, then goes towards the counter to get her keys. I give her a smile and a quick wave before returning to my syllabus as the door closes behind them.

I love Physics, I really do. While most people are good at Art and English, I'm really good at Math and Science in school. Sure, I played soccer too, but this is my thing. I'd been a science fair champ, and my dad came to every single one. Sometimes I wish I had similar projects now, but college doesn't do science fairs, so I'm stuck. Lab is fun, but they aren't super experimental in community college—they just exist. I get an assignment and I have to do what's on the paper or I fail, basically. Where's the fun in that?

But it doesn't matter.

It's not really worth it anymore.

I just need my degree. That's it.

I'm struggling to get through my English syllabus when Austin bursts into the dining space after sprinting down the hall.

"Are you ready?!" He exclaims, "Riley and the others just texted that they were on their way and I don't wanna be late!"

"You can wait two seconds," I reply.

"Not when we have to walk. I don't understand why we can't just drive anymore." he states.

"If you wanted to be driven you should've asked mom," I say coldly, getting up to put my shoes on. He knows full well why I can't drive him anywhere. "Besides, walking is good for you."

He groans as I finish putting my things in my bag. "Come on!" he whines.

"I thought my brother was sixteen, not six" I laugh. He brushes past me, purposely bumping my shoulders as we leave and I lock the door behind us.

During the walk, Austin is either talking about his friends or pulling my arm to go faster, and if we went any faster we'd be running. I get the hint that he likes Riley from the way he talks about her. He seems like he just wants to see her. It's kinda sweet. I was the same way and apparently Dad did that with Mom. I guess it just runs in the family.

The walk is familiar, muscle memory, at this point. We start near the apartment by the highway, where the cars never really sleep, and head toward the quieter parts of Ivywood. Austin drags me past the park he used to play at and the cemetery he refuses to walk through alone, even though he claims he's not scared of anything. His school sits just up the road, brick and boring, but he still points it out like I might forget it exists. The farther we go, the more the town opens up, like it's finally waking up too.

It's also nice to see him not hanging out with the baseball team. I'm not a big fan of them, they can be jerks sometimes, but Austin loves 'em, so who am I to tell him they suck? Though his friends outside of baseball are really sweet, Riley is new.

When we finally make it to the Beanstalk Bistro, Austin speedwalks away from the door to his friends immediately. I set my things down at a table on the other side of the room, just to give him space.

I'm not sure how long I'm sitting here, dazed by the job applications and syllabi once more, but I'm brought back to the real world by Vincent shutting my computer.

"I was just gonna take your order, but something's off." He laughs. "What's goin' on?"

"You never have to take my order, you know me," I say with a sarcastic smile. He gives me a knowing look and I hesitate before answering, "I—I don't know...:" Vincent remains quiet, so I continue.

"It's just... I had to help Mom pay the rent last month... So I'm looking for another job."

"Another? Payton, you already have two." He scoffs.

"It's not enough."

"I can't stop you from trying, can I..?" He asks.

I shake my head as the bell above the door rings.

"Look, if you really need the money, talk to your managers. Use the college student card, it might work." He laughs. "And if all else fails, I can try to make space for you here."

"Thanks Vin...I'll get back to ya."

"No prob. Gotta go!" He says, shooting me a finger gun and making a "pow" sound.

I reopen my computer to see the Indeed page again. I contemplate just applying for everything I can find but choose to just close out the tab instead. Maybe I can just talk to my manager at the rink, maybe he'll understand?

Who knows.

chapter two

As much as I like my job, I get so bored sometimes. When school is in session, the busiest times of the day are when the Early College gym class comes in at 9:00 A.M. or when couples come in at night.

But it's night and there is not a single couple in sight. At this point, I'm just waiting 'til 11:00 P.M. which means I have thirty minutes or so left to kill.

I go to the lockers behind me and grab my bag, mostly just for my computer.

When I open it, the slides from my music class appear. Today's slides were mostly about the business side of things and publishing. It's honestly pretty cool.

Music is something I really enjoy—I have the highest minutes out of everyone on my Spotify Wrapped, and my dad was in a band when he was younger. He played the drums, and he got me into it as well, it was our favorite way to bond. I still have the cassette tape of their music and the drum set he got me, keeping it with me to comfort me on rough days.

So needless to say, it gets a lot of use these days.

I close out the school and job tabs, since it's Friday, and for once in my life I don't have any work to do. My raise is being processed, thank god, so I can quit the job search. Once the tabs are all gone, I slightly jump seeing the words **The Vermont Resilience Institute** appear. I take a peek around the corners of the front desk.

No one's here... It can't hurt to check. I think to myself.

Still, I lower my screen brightness even if it makes me squint, just to hide what I'm looking at.

I slide my mouse across the top of the page.

Our Team Members!

I click it.

A giant list of people all in different categories come up.

Addiction Therapists, Behavioral, Divorce, Eating Disorder Therapists, Marriage and Family

Counselors, Psychiatrists, even Pastoral. "Trauma Therapists" makes a lump form in my throat. I *know* that's what mom wanted me to look at. I click on that next.

A bunch of maybe fifteen pictures of smiling faces pop up. All the names are in alphabetical order by first name, which throws me off. Why do it that way when we've all been put in alphabetical order by last name our whole lives? I mean, I'm sure it doesn't matter to anyone else but me, but still.

Scrolling through the website, names and bios appear, and even the categories have sub-categories, making my head spin.

I go through all of them and I see Art Therapy, CPT, TF-CBT, and then I pause.

CBT & Narrative Exposure Therapy

I look at the screen for a few seconds, hesitating to keep diving. I could feel myself start to shake when I heard music lightly playing from one of the rinks and slamming my computer shut.

I look back at the time.

10:50 P.M.

I've been here for twenty minutes..?

Shaking the thoughts away, I start towards the rink.

No one should be here right now anyways. I didn't see anyone come in. How long have they been here? I push the door open and before I can say anything the sound of an Alec Benjamin song overcomes me. My eyes are drawn to this figure gliding across the ice like it's the easiest thing in the world.

I can't help but quietly move closer to the glass as the bridge of what I think is "Devil Doesn't Bargain" plays. Their hair is in tight coils, pulled back into a puffy ponytail with two small braids. From what I can see, their skin is speckled with small patches of vitiligo. They're covered, from head to toe in pastel yellow and white, with a yellow cropped sweater and skirt, white leggings and skates, and yellow legwarmers.

They turn and I catch a glimpse of their eyes, when theirs lock on mine.

Soft green eyes. They're pretty.

And familiar.

I think they recognize me too when I see the shock on their face before the pick of their skate catches on the ice, bringing them down mid-spin.

There's no way I'm filling out more paperwork this close to close... but I care, so I run over to her to make sure she's not hurt.

"Sorry!" they laugh, "Am I not supposed to be here?"

I look up and see the rim of my hat, which I rip off.

"I mean—no... But that doesn't matter. Are you alright?" I ask, extending a hand.

They take it as they go, "Yeah, nothing I haven't done before." They fixed their footing. "I'm very clumsy."

"You made it look so easy."

"Eh, years of practice'll do that."

There's an awkward silence. "This is going to sound weird but, have we met before?" they ask.

"I think so—I think you bumped into me once at the bistro..."

They perk up as their face goes red. "That was you!? Oh my gosh, I'm still so sorry."

"It's still fine." I snicker.

I watch as they look me up and down, stopping at my shoes. "What...are those?"

Looking down, as if I forgot what I had on, I say, "I can't skate so—I wear these. Slip resistant."

"They're monstrosities." They laugh again, "I'm Jada, by the way." He extends his hand, smiling.

"I'm Payton."

chapter three

I've been seeing Jada a lot. I'm not sure why but somehow wherever I am, they are too. The rink doesn't count—I expect them to be there. But the bistro, *and* the park, *and* the record shop? All at the same time as me?

That's weird. Right?

Like, I'm not crazy, am I?

They came in today to practice during my shift. I just clocked out and now we're sitting together. It's quiet. They've got a hot chocolate from the concessions bar. It's made with water.

"I still can't believe you don't like this," she says.

"I can't believe you do. Hot chocolate should be made with milk."

"I do it like this at home too!" She laughs.

"Anyone who does that, at home, *by choice,* is crazy." I mean that with my full chest. Why on earth would you have chocolate water... It's flavored HOT water! I know this is a stupid thing to get upset over, but come on. "So, speaking of home, where are you from?"

He gives me a somewhat conflicted look.

"What? What's with the face?"

"I'm honestly from all over..?" he replies vaguely.

"Military?"

"No, business women for mothers." He laughs, "My moms aren't separated but they live in two different countries for their company."

That's cool."Where?"

"I'm originally from Canada and that's where my mother lives, and my mum lives in the UK. I also lived with my older brother for two years in France!" he smiles."My brother is a music producer now and he mostly works with international artists. I did a study abroad program in high school, so I got to live with him!"

I start to try and ask about his family as he keeps going on about his brother and sister. Apparently, Tristan, his brother, isn't just a producer but he also makes his own music and he's a photographer. His sister, Tia, is a paramedic and studying to be a nurse.

They mostly just rave on about their siblings before even coming close to talking about themself.

"So, Canada, huh?" I laugh.

"Yeah, I didn't think I'd end up here," they say, picking at the rim of the cup. "Vermont, I mean. It's so... not Ottawa."

I nod. "What made you choose Golden Sierra?"

They hesitate. "It's a long story."

"What *isn't* a long story? We've got time," I say, easy but encouraging.

She glanced out the window, watching the lights from passing cars blur into streaks of color. "I mean, my parents suggested it. Opportunities and stuff. I mean, America is the leading country in higher education," she started, hesitating on what to say next,

"I guess...I just needed a fresh start. Somewhere new. Somewhere I could figure things out without everyone I grew up with watching."

I nod again. "Makes sense. Vermont's good for that, I think."

"Yeah," she says, smiling softly. "Well, so far, so good. Honestly, it's mostly just adjusting. New town, new country...new life."

"Can't be easy."

"Pretty standard for me, actually. But this is the first time I've done it without my parents. I've moved between countries twice before, but this is the first time I've done this by myself. I have to admit, it's quite nice being able to do this, mostly, all on my own. And the scholarships are great."

I chuckled, raising an eyebrow. "About that...what do you even do at GSA? I know they don't have anything for skating."

"They don't have to. I don't plan on it being my future," she says.

She says it so casually I nearly choke on my drink. "Seriously? But you're amazing at this—why would you waste time on it and not use it in your future?"

"You sound like my parents," she says, seemingly forcing a smile. "I'm a dance major, and I'll be a secondary education minor once I finish my gen-eds. I'm going to study to be a teacher, mostly a dance teacher. So I wouldn't say it's a waste." She sighs, annoyed.

I soften as I fumble for a response. I sound like such an asshole right now. "I'm sorry—that's not what—I didn't mean it like that…" I stutter…*oh my god*. "It's not a waste; it's just surprising. You're so good at this. I'm shocked you'd do anything else."

"I've been dancing my whole life. Doing it on ice is just something for fun. I've always wanted to teach others, though. I want to be the inspiration for a new generation. I can do that as a teacher."

"I guess that makes sense," I admit, nodding.

"But it doesn't matter much anyways," he says, dejected, "American Academy is a lot more expensive than Canadian or European University…and as well off as my family is, I may not be able to get help paying for next year."

"I thought you had scholarships?"

"One for dance ensemble, which is $2,000 and one for the teachers association, which for me is a minor, making it $2,000 as well. The rest is paid by my family and $26,000 is a lot of money that I just don't have." He pulls out his computer and starts typing, before turning it to me.

"Wasn't school here their idea? Why would they have you come here if they weren't gonna help keep you here?"

"I don't know. My siblings had to pay for school on their own, too, so it's nothing new...But I've applied for every scholarship I qualify for and I've not gotten any of them, and I don't qualify for the FAFSA because I'm an 'International Student', and the CSLP doesn't give me anything."

I watch him sink into his chair as he turns his computer back around. I'm not sure why, but I feel just as upset as he does. At least, as sad as the feeling I see in his eyes. He's not hard to read, every time I see him, I can easily tell what he's feeling based on nothing but a 'hello'.

I take a look around the rink, scanning the walls.

"What?" she says, straight faced. My eyes finally land on a poster stuck on the middle column wall. I walk towards it and rip it off.

I sit back down and slide it onto the table.

"What is this?" She picks up the poster, reading it.

"This is 'The National American Ice-Dancing Competition'. It might be able to help you if you win."

"The what?" She reads, "First place gets...$80,000?!" she whispers, shocked. "That could pay for the next 3 years!" she smiles, then her smile falters. "But that—Payton, that's a very big if."

"With your skill? I think it's possible. And even if you get second or third, you still win enough to pay for the next year or two."

She sinks back down into her chair.

"Even so I don't think that—"

"Listen, you can keep applying for scholarships and try to get a campus job or something, but it's worth a shot...right?"

"Perchance..." She sighs, grabbing her phone.

"You can't just say 'perchance."

"I say 'perchance'," she says, letting out a soft chuckle.

And after a quick google search, because we aren't crazy...she's in.

chapter four

"Five skates please!" Austin shouts over the music. Today is a Friday, so needless to say I am not getting out of here on time.

"That's $50."

"Come on, no discount cause we're family?" he half-jokes, giving me puppy dog eyes.

I keep my deadpan. "Those have never worked on me and you know it."

He groans dramatically, giving me five $10's wrapped in a rubber band. His friends walk up to my coworker to get their wristbands, and Austin hangs back.

"What, did you walk here? Isn't mom at work?" I ask.

"Mom got out early so she drove us here!" He exclaimed. He gets so happy when mom does literally anything. "She promised she'd take us to get dinner later too!" It's how he gets let down.

Look, I love my mom. I really do. But ever since...last year...she's made promises she never keeps. She's always busy with work, every time she gets home I'm doing my homework in the kitchen taking care of *her* kids. Millie is my *little sister*, not my baby. It's why Ashleigh is always at the house. She's the one taking care of Millie when Austin is out and I'm at work. Not mom. Ashleigh is sweet, but like mom said, she has a life. She can't spend all her afternoons watching Millie. She probably still would be there if mom didn't get off early.

How do you even get out early working in the maternity ward?

Guess it's no one's birthday today.

"Oh, also mom wants to pick you up today. She's getting the car cleaned," Austin says, taking back what he said when he sees me tense up.

I hate the car. I hate being anywhere *near* the inside of a motor vehicle.

I don't do 'driving' and I don't do cars.

She *knows* this.

She knows this better than anyone.

Before I can shake my head no or even say the words, Austin moves his hand up, slightly waving it.

"Never mind. I'll text her." He smiles.

I can't help but smile back. How can I not? He knows me better than I think I know myself, and vice versa. From just one look he knows exactly what I'm feeling.

Which is why I saw his face light up when I looked at Jada when they appeared in the window of the second rink.

"Who...was that?" He grinned.

"That's Jada. She's...my friend? Why?"

"You made a friend..? Like, on your own?!" he stuttered, seemingly holding in a laugh.

"You act like I've never made friends before," I stammered.

"I mean—"

"I have friends!" I yelled, a bit too loud.

"How dare you assume I think you don't! You should never assume." He puts on a smug little smirk as he continues, "Now if you'll excuse me, I'm gonna go see mine," and he turns, running down the hall. "Byeeeee!"

I'd yell at him for running but I just don't care.

Turning to my coworker, I ask her to cover me while I check the second rink.

I quickly get to the door of the rink, a little too quickly, and watch as they try to figure out a routine. A few twirls, something where they glide for a bit holding their skate, and then they try this jump with a spin and while I open the door, they land hard.

Like, it looks like it hurts.

They got back up immediately, so I didn't have to worry about them being hurt, or paperwork that would've come with it, which is nice. But the only thing I could think of to say is, "So—how's it goin'—?", a bit sarcastically, which gets me a glare.

I continue walking towards the rim, watching as she slowly glides around the rink.

"I cannot figure this out. I know the move, I've done something similar before," they say, frustrated, "I don't know exactly what's changed." They land right in front of me on the other side of the rim, lightly tapping their toe pick into the ice.

"Do you have a video?" I ask.

"Of what?"

"That spin you tried."

"Why?" they asked, skeptical.

"Maybe I can help."

He snorts and says, "No offense but... how would you be able to help..? You can't skate."

"Math is a key part in many sports, and so is physics. No matter how much you hate it, you're always doing it." I laugh, "But, lucky for you, I happen to be pretty good at both of those."

He takes a second, tapping his toe pick into the ice a bit faster, sighing, and walking off the rink to get his phone.

"Here." He pulls up a YouTube video of this guy from 2008 competing. "I don't know what they're saying but you should be able to recognize what I was trying." He laughs, gliding back onto the ice. The voice over is in Japanese, which honestly is pretty nice. I haven't spoken it in a while so it's a good test to see what I remember.

*. ❄ * ❄ *. ❄ .* ❄ * ❄ .*

I got to take my break and I think I've watched this thing about thirty times and I have almost three full note pages. Slowing it down, stopping it in different spots, watching this guy's movements. His name is Yuzuru Hanyu and he is fantastic. I googled him and apparently he's universally thought of as one of the greatest figure skaters in history.

He is a two-time World champion, six-time Japanese national champion, and the first single skater to win four consecutive Grand Prix Finals.

He is also the first and only single skater to be ranked first in the ISU World Standings for five consecutive seasons.

Hanyu broke world records nineteen times, *and*, this is the most important one, he was the first skater to land a quadruple loop jump in international competition, among *many* other things.

Basically this is the kinda guy you'd have posters on your wall of.

What Jada wants to do is called a Triple Axel which is this guy's signature move.

A move only twenty-seven people, including Hanyu, have landed.

Jada purposefully slams into the rink wall, making me jump in my seat. "How's it goin'?" They smile.

"This guy is amazing, very skilled. I'm gonna need more time with it, but I can figure it out."

"That's alright, I think I'm done for today anyways," they say, stepping off the rink and sitting a seat away from me.

It's quiet. A bit too quiet as they take off their skates. I keep thinking about how shocked Austin was when I told him Jada was my friend. I know I don't talk to people much or do anything but work, for that matter, but is it *really* that hard to believe?

Come to think of it, I've never hung out with Jada outside of the rink. I don't even think I have their phone number.

I look over to her as she puts the guards on her skates. "Hey…" I croak.

"Yea?" She looks over. "What's up?"

"Do you, I don't know… wanna go to dinner? With me?" I clear my throat, "Like, after I get out of work?"

I see her slightly blank stare when I ask and I start, "Never mind, I'll just see you next—"

"No!" She exclaims, "I mean, yes! I'd like to hang out with you." She smiles.

"C-cool! Yeah, I'm done at like…five? If you wanna wait?"

"Sure thing!" she chirped, shuffling out and to the common area between the rinks.

*. ❄ * ❄ *. ❄ .* ❄ * ❄ .*

Once I clocked out, and told Austin I was leaving, we went to town. Main Street is always pretty

nice to walk down, but at night? It's *beautiful*. All of
the shops, restaurants, the bistro, and the sidewalks are
lined with warm lights, and there are musicians on
every other corner, helping attract people inside.

I glance over and Jada's got her hands in her
pockets, but her eyes are basically glowing with
anticipation as we walk down Main Street.

"I've been meaning to come here for a while,"
she finally says.

"What kept you?"

"Classes, I'm *always* so busy!" she exclaims
with a chuckle.

"Better late than never?" I shrug, taking off my
jacket. "It's fall now, why is it so hot?"

She looks towards me. "Technically, autumn
doesn't start until the 23rd this year, it's only the 15th."
Then she smiles wide. "Nice tattoo!"

"Thanks, I've been meaning to get another
one. I just don't know what to get yet."

"I want one someday but, I do ballet so that's already a no, and it's hard enough to find a shade that matches my skin tone." They laugh.

"I didn't know they were that strict."

"It really depends on the place but the dance team is strict about it."

I give a thumbs down. "Boo, no fun."

"Y'know, the more I look at it, the more it looks like a DNA strand," they guess.

"That was on purpose." I started, "'Cause—uhm, I really like music and I really like plants, so...Y'know they like—intertwine?"

It gets quiet again.

I'm awful at this.

I look for anything, anything at all to try and start up some conversation again.

"I—uhm—I like your necklace," I blurt out.

"What?" they look down, "Oh! Thank you, I forgot which one I had on."

"That's a citrine, right?"

"Yes! I love crystals! I collect them and I've made so many necklaces with them, mostly yellow of course. I didn't know you liked crystals."

"It was one of the units I enjoyed in my earth sciences class," I say.

She started rambling on about her favorite crystals: Alexandrite, Painite, Lapis lazuli, Agate, and Yellow Citrine. She also really likes Bumblebee Jasper, but she hasn't found any yet.

"I love making jewelry with the ones I find too. I used to sell them on Etsy." He smiles. "I would give them one based on their vibe."

"What would you give me?" I ask.

He stops us for a second, looks me up and down. Placing his hands on my shoulders, he pushes down a bit, meeting my eyes.

"What are you doing..?" I hesitate when he shushes me before saying, "Blue Kyanite."

"Why?"

"I don't know, it's the *vibe*," he hints. "Google the throat chakra," he whispers, excitedly. "Besides,

with a thinner silver chain it would look really good."
He makes a photo frame with his hands. "Yeah, I see it.
Now I've got to find one." He laughs again.

He's about to turn around when I see him
hesitate. "What happened there..?" I watch his eyes
shift from wonder to concern, looking to the side of
my neck as the question sends a shiver up my spine. My
bones and whatever muscle I have feels loose. Before he
says anything else, I glance over to the building right
next to us. The Tokyo Table. "Let's eat there," I choke
out.

"Oh—um...sure?" he falters, breaking his gaze
and starting towards the door. I follow as a pit forms in
my stomach, then slowly gets a bit worse as we step
inside. It smells amazing, ramen broth and chicken
wafting through the air. But food and anxiety don't
mix well. Jada goes up to the counter to get us a table. I
haven't been here in ages.

*. ❄ * ❄ *. ❄ * ❄ * ❄ .*

I end up getting sushi, Uramaki Dragon Roll
and Temaki Soft Shell Crab. It's somehow easier on my
stomach.

I always love it here. My family and I would come all the time. It's owned by a family from Japan, so the food is all authentic, which is great when your dad is the one who cooks at home. He hated eating Japanese food out unless it was here. Honestly, he was right, anywhere else sucks. We used to make everything at home together. But nothing beat his homemade ramen. The days he'd make it, the house would be filled to the brim with the smell of chicken broth and spices. Even the neighbors would say something about it, all good things, of course.

When they bring out Jada's ramen, I nearly melt. "Now that—smells amazing." I grin. "It smells nearly identical to my dad's."

"You make ramen at home?"

"We used to, now anyone who can cook is usually too busy." I add, "Besides, I can't find dad's recipe."

"Can you say that again?" they ask.

"Say what again—?"

"How do you say 'can't?'" they coax, holding back a laugh.

"C*ai*n't?" I say, puzzled.

"You—" they laugh, "You get an accent on specific words."

"You have an accent all the time!" I object, my accent becoming more significant.

"Yes, but that's because I grew up all around it. But half the time when you natter on, I hear tiny twinges of it. Where do you get that from?"

"I'm from Texas," I say. "Born and raised, 10 years." They laugh again. "What? What's so funny?" I prod.

"No, you just don't give off that southern vibe. At least not *that* southern," they banter.

"Ok fine, but 'natter'? Where the hell are you from where that's a normal word in conversation?" I tease.

"I'll have you know, I got that from my friends in the UK, thank you very much."

"Whatever." I laugh. "It's more tellin' when I'm mad."

"Or when you say the word '*telling*." They joke, eating their ramen.

Y'know, I used to hate my accent being mocked. It's why it's not very telling that I even have one, I hide it on purpose. But this doesn't bother me. I can't help but laugh with them. Who am I right now?

chapter five

I adore the Bistro. It's quiet, it's calm, I can just do my work and have my coffee, as soon as it gets here, without having to worry about those around me. But right now...It's too quiet.

And that's when the door bursts open and a few seconds later, my laptop is being slammed shut.

"You are never going to believe this!" Jada yells, drawing the attention of the rest of the bistro to the table. I barely have time to greet her before she slaps a paper down in front of me. "Look at this."

I blink, glancing at the faded newsprint. **"Jacqueline Knight: The First Black Gay Woman to Win the National American Ice-Dancing Competition."**

I look back up at Jada. "Wait—who is that?"

Jada grins, tapping the article. "It's my mom! She won in 1993 and I had no idea. I was searching up the event after we talked and found this." They shake their head, half in disbelief, half in pride. "She never told me."

"Seriously?" I frown. "Why wouldn't she mention something like this?"

"I dunno," she admits, still staring at the article. "But I printed it out so I could ask her later. Look at this part."

Her finger traces a paragraph near the bottom. I lean in to read.

"...the competition's climax was nearly overshadowed by controversy when Knight executed a risky triple axel in the final stretch of the performance. The move, known for its difficulty and high injury risk, nearly cost her the win in 1993's 70th Annual Competition..."

I let out a low whistle. "Damn. That's intense. Isn't that the move you were trying to do?"

Jada nods. "Yeah. It was even debated for a ban, but they never followed through."

I glance at her, catching the way her eyes shone with something I didn't like. Determination. Ambition. The kind that led to bad decisions.

"You're not thinking of still doing it... are you?"

"I should try my hardest since it's the 100th Annual," he says, starting with a bright smile. "Right? Make it special."

I set my coffee down, crossing my arms. "Jada, that move is dangerous."

"So is walking down a flight of stairs," he teases, smiling, "if you're not paying attention."

"Don't do that."

"Do what?"

"Act like that move is the same as tripping on the sidewalk," I shoot back. "If it almost cost your mom the win, what makes you think it won't do the same to you?"

"Because I'll land it," he says simply.

I sigh, running a hand through my hair. "I've looked up this move. Only twenty-seven people, including Hanyu, have landed it. You might not become the twenty-eighth. I don't like this."

"You don't have to," Jada replies, playful but firm. "Besides, doing this would mean the world to me!"

I huff, "You do seem more excited about it." I move my computer to the side, "Why? I mean, it's going to help you pay for college if you win, that's great. But what else?"

"So—how do I say this?" he starts, "It would be a great way to get closer to my mom."

"Rocky relationship?" I ask, moving my chair closer to the table.

"Not really...I'm adopted," he whispered, "And like, don't get me wrong, I've never felt like I'm not part of the family or anything, they're amazing. But there's always this...I don't know, this feeling that there's...this gap between my siblings and I?" He shrinks into his seat a bit, "It's dumb, but I want to feel like I really belong there."

"Well—uhm—" I begin, "I guess...I can help you with whatever you need."

He looks up towards me, a smile spreading across his face.

"I wouldn't listen to him if I were you," a voice says, coming up as she sets my coffee down on the table.

I feel my whole body go rigid as Jada and I turn to her in unison, and there she is.

She stands with a slight slouch, throwing a rag in one hand over her shoulder, replacing it with a note pad and a pencil. She looks almost bored, but her eyes—a light brown, glowing like fiery embers in the bistro's warm light—are sharp. Studying us. She is small—shorter than Jada, shorter than me—but there is something about her presence that makes her feel taller. Maybe it is the way she holds herself. The casual confidence. Or maybe it is the streaks of red in her dark curls, catching the light as she tilts her head. Whatever it is, I feel the same discomfort settle in my chest that I always do when she is around.

Jada, however, just frowns slightly. "And you are?"

Her lips curl into a smile, but it doesn't quite reach her eyes. "Viviana, we go to school together." She put the pencil behind her ear, wiping her hand on her apron. "I also work here."

Jada glances at me, then back at her. "Right...the tutor. I'm Jada..." they start, "Nice to meet you, I guess," they whisper under their breath. That usually gets a laugh out of me.

Viviana ignores that, looking at the paper still spread across the table. "You're training for NAI-DC?"

"Something like that," Jada answers cautiously.

Viviana nods, like she already knew the answer. Then she turns her attention to me, and the temperature in the room seems to drop by a few degrees. "And you're the one helping them?"

I clench my jaw. "I mean—" I clear my throat, "we're just talking and—" Her eyes flicker with something unreadable before she turns back to Jada, her expression smoothing into something almost friendly. *Almost.* "If you want *real* help," she says, interrupting me, "you should practice with someone else."

Jada shifts, frowning. "No offense, but why would I do that? What gives you the right to—"

"Payton's not the best person to ask for help," she says smoothly. "Speaking from...experience."

"Just leave us alone," I interrupt, looking down towards the paper, then to Jada.

Jada hesitates, but only for a moment. Then they cross their arms. "I appreciate the advice, but I'm good."

For the first time, something in Viviana's expression wavers. She recovers quickly, but I didn't miss the way her jaw tensed, or the slight flash of irritation in her eyes before she smiled again. This time, there's an edge to it.

"Just, be careful," she says, then clearing her throat, "Are you ordering anything?" she asks, grabbing her pencil.

"No. Thanks." Jada puffs, shrugging and turning away.

Jada lets out a low breath as Viviana disappears into the back. "Well, that was...something."

I exhale, willing my shoulders to relax. "Yeah."

"Anyways, I was thinking Friday? After you're done with work?"

"Um...yeah, sure. That works." I nod hesitantly.

chapter six

I hate getting out of work late. I love the walk home, but on days like this—where I have to be the parent—it sucks.

I scan my door key and start towards the elevator, where I have to scan my key again which is so idiotic. I already did it to get into the building, we know I live here. I live on the eighth floor, two from the top. I press the button and the doors shut, leaving me in the silence.

My earbuds are still in and playing my favorite song at the moment, "Iris" by The Goo Goo Dolls. I swear, this building has the slowest elevator. I'm allowed to hate on it—my dad built it. I do what I like, and in the slow, nearly quiet stillness, I see something sparkle out of the corner of my eye.

A gold ring with an orange gem.

Picking it up, the small engraving on the inside grazes my fingertips.

It's Viviana's. I remember when she lost this, her dad got it for her before he was deployed, and she didn't stop crying for hours...but he's back...and she's got the real thing now.

I pocket the ring and enter my apartment.

As soon as I open the door, the room that used to smell of mom's favorite peach scented candle, now smells of popcorn and doritos as the voice of Neil deGrasse Tyson fills the house. A voice I know all too well. So much so I know exactly what Austin is watching: *Cosmos: A Spacetime Odyssey.*

"I'm home!" I announce, trying to make sure Austin hears me over the TV as I take off my shoes and put my work bag on the rack. "Turn that down will you? Where's Millie?"

"Sleeping," he says, tuned out.

"Ok, where's mom?"

"Work."

"Can you answer with more than one word?"

"Of course." He smiles, smugly leaning over the back of the couch. "I made popcorn!"

"I can see that, have you eaten?"

"Pop. Corn," he emphasizes, waving the bowl in my face.

"I'll take that as a no." I sigh, starting towards the kitchen. As much as I want to be upset with him for not making himself food, I can't. I'd be a hypocrite. "How do you feel about a bowl?"

"Taco Bowls!? Let's go!!" he yells, wrapping up the chips and cleaning up his notebooks, then throwing himself off the couch to join me in the kitchen, speed walking up to help me with it, pulling his sock up along the way.

He grabs the black beans, olives, cheese, chipotle ranch, and sour cream from the fridge as I start on the chicken and rice.

This is one of maybe three things I know how to cook. Austin calls this "my specialty".

I call it "easy".

Especially when I'm the one taking care of him most days, even before dad...yeah. Anyways, it's good to have quick things to make just to make things easier on the both of us.

As I finish up, I grab an avocado for my bowl, watching Austin physically recoil while I tease putting some into his.

.❄❉*. ❄ .*❉*❄.*

About two hours later, I'm trying to get my homework done so that all I have to worry about tomorrow is the work I get paid to do.

Austin is working on his homework while he plays Voltron on the TV. I don't know how he works like this. It's hard enough to work with all these tabs open and he's listening to Keith and Lance flirt with each other like it's the end of the world.

I start getting rid of tabs when my computer cast "divine light". I hit the brightness when I notice the screen.

CBT & Narrative Exposure Therapy

I look at the screen for a few seconds, hesitating to do anything, when, "Hey, Payt—" rings through my ears, making me slam my computer shut.

I forgot I left that tab open.

"Damn, man, it's just homework." Austin laughs.

"Sorry—I just—"

"You're good. Can you help me with my history homework?"

"For the love of Archimedes—" I hiss under my breath, "you know I'm not good at—"

"Well neither am I," he interrupts," so I figured two is better than one!" He smiles nervously.

I can't stand him sometimes. He's lucky I love him. "Sit down." I sigh.

As I move my things to the side, he eagerly pulls out the chair and sits with me, slowly moving the chair closer. We end up sitting here for about an hour as I help him make flashcards based on the reading while we start listening to one of his David Bowie vinyls.

I give him a practice quiz so I can get back to my homework. Dad used to give me practice quizzes with History and English—they were my worst subjects growing up. I think I still have my old flashcards somewhere in my room hidden in a drawer. I don't know…I blocked out anything from high school, not thinking about it much anymore.

Austin slides the paper my way and I "grade" it for the next two hours.

Austin falls asleep next to me, while I'm grading. I give him my jacket. I lightly push him to wake him up. "Hey, you passed."

"Yayyy," he says, sleepily.

"Go to bed. I'll put this back in your bag."

Austin leaves, taking my jacket with him.

I reopen my computer, switching tabs as soon as I open it, continuing my homework.

*. ❄ * ❄ *. ❄ .* ❄ * ❄ .*

By 2:30 A.M., I hear the door slowly creak as I close my laptop, which means Mom just got back.

Glancing up, I see her expression drop as she clicks the door shut behind her

"Why are you still up?" she asks.

"I had homework," I whisper, bluntly.

I just ask her how work was and tell her there's leftovers in the fridge if she wants anything. I hear her trying to get my attention as I walk back to my room, ignoring her worry and her whispered yells, asking why I wasn't asleep earlier.

I just go to my room, tired. It's suddenly way too quiet.

Setting my computer down on my desk and my bag in my desk chair, I grab my headphones and the remote to my fairy light LED's.

I set it to a cool blue, changing into my pj's, shorts and a hoodie, before putting my headphones on.

I just lay in bed and stay awake for another hour, thinking as "The View Between Villages" by Noah Kahan—extended, of course— echos through my brain.

chapter seven

Friday. Sometimes I love Friday. Especially
when I don't have work.

Even if I still have to be at the rink with Jada,
it's better than having to put on a fake smile for the
people who come in and don't even bother to smile
back. Like—I can *not* smile. But apparently that's rude.
But it's *not* rude for them not to smile or be nice?
Whatever.

None of that matters today.

Jada runs in, nearly out of breath.

"You're late." I laugh.

"I know, I know!" She pants. "Sorry."

"It's ok. You said you had something to show
me?"

She looks at me, confused.

"Some video?" I say.

"Oh! Right!" She throws her things down next to the bleacher, sitting down and taking her phone out of her mini yellow purse. "I was doing some more digging after I showed you that newspaper, and found this!"

She scoots closer to me and hooks one of her arms through mine, offering me an earbud.

"I Have Nothing" by Whitney Houston begins to play as he starts the video, a girl appearing. She's dressed from head to toe in performance attire. A sparkly, light green dress, brown tights, and white skates with a small pink charm on them. Her braids are up in a ponytail that is braided into a bigger braid and wrapped up in a bun. That's some commitment, I can barely go get a retwist much less keep braids that nice.

As she starts to skate I ask, "Who's this again?"

"That's my mom!" he exclaims, slightly shaking me in excitement.

I make it a point to say that she's incredibly talented, just watching her I can tell that she probably practiced like it was the end of the world. Every movement was just so. It was clean and beautiful.

It's no wonder she won that year.

"That's pretty cool," I say, "Can you send me this?"

"Yeah!"

He unloops his arm and sends me the video while I grab my notebook and pen. "So I have a plan. It's not going to be easy, but it can work."

I let them read my notes, but it looks more like they skimmed them. "It's still incredibly dangerous."

"You are so overly cautious!" They laugh.

"For good reason—"

"Come on, Payt!" they cut me off. 'Payt?'

"I—no—We can do this! Maybe I can even teach you to skate!" They laugh. "Then you can get rid of those god awful shoes."

"I don't know, Jada—"

"You said you'd help me if I needed it."

They stare at me, somewhat longingly, with puppy-dog eyes.

I sigh. "Alright, let's do this..."

I don't know what I just signed up for, but it's not like I can back out now.

quarter 2

""All it takes is a beautiful fake smile to hide an injured soul."

- Robin Williams

chapter eight

I really admire their passion. Every single day, they fall, get back up, and try again. Jada is stubbornly inspiring, and it's annoying.

Especially because they aren't doing anything wrong, so they're just messing up because of their own doubts at this point. The math worked. The angles, the momentum—it was all right. And yet, they still hesitated. They still cut themself short, hitting the wall before they could make the turn.

From my seat, I watch Jada launch into a spin. Their blades scrape against the ice in a fluid rhythm before they stumble, the motion faltering slightly. They recover quickly, but their muttered frustration echoes faintly across the rink. I admit, I really do admire their determination. It was the kind of persistence I respect. My fingers twitch over my sketchbook page that's half-filled with a rough sketch of Jada mid-spin.

But even with all of this, watching her, I get more excited about helping her. I'm scared for her every time she falls, but I still *want* to be here.

It's weird, really. This doesn't feel like a chore to me.

"You're overthinking it," I yell to her, moving closer. Sitting on the bench near the ice, I put my sketchbook down and scroll through my phone to review the footage of today's practice.

Jada huffs, skating over to where I'm sitting. "I am not overthinking it."

"You are," I say without looking up. "You hesitate at the last second. That's the only reason it's not working."

Jada groans and leans over the boards. "Well, excuse me for not wanting to die."

I smirk. "You won't die. Worst case, you fall."

"I *have* been falling."

"Then what's one more?" I grin as Jada scowls playfully, sticking out her tongue.

She watches as I scroll through slow-motion replays of her routine. "Alright, genius," she says, "If you think it's so easy, why don't you try it?"

I raise an eyebrow. "What?"

Jada smirks, starting towards the door. "You spend so much time analyzing everything. Maybe it'd help if you actually got on the ice."

Before I could start my protest she'd already left to grab a pair of skates.

When she gets back she holds them up, proudly. "I got you a men's eight? And they're blue!" she smiles.

"Jada—" I sighed, "I don't think this is a good idea—"

"You won' t know til' you try!" he smiled, "Come on, please?"

And before I know it, I'm putting the skates on.

I'm not exactly sure why I feel bad saying "no" to him. I know when to say no—my boundaries are usually pretty inflexible—but with small things like this, I find it hard to just say "no". I'm also not sure why I can't lace these damn things up. I do this all the time for other kids, what's the problem here? It shouldn't be any different on my own.

Jada comes over, "What are you, stalling?" he laughs. "Here let me—" kneeling down, his expression throws off. "What's that..?"

"What—"

"The metal rods?" he interrupts, slight concern in his voice.

I hesitate before tugging up my jeans. The fabric catches on the brace strapped to my leg, and when it finally clears, the scars are there—raised and pale, twisting across my skin like lightning frozen mid-strike. The brace glints under the light, strapped over a leg carved with scars. Ugly ones. The kind that make people unable to decide if they want to stare or look away.

Jada just stares.

"It's my brace... I was in an accident a while back. It helps me."

"And you were just-"

I interrupt him, "It's no different from you and your knee brace." I push my jeans back down and start trying to tie the laces again.

"You- you don't have to if you don't want to... I'm sorry for pushing, I didn't—"

"Exactly, you didn't know. Most people don't and I'd like to keep it that way. So—" I sigh. "Are we doing this or what?"

Jada smiles, helps me finish tying the laces, and says, "you bet." He helps me up as I stumble.

This is embarrassing.

"Take it slow. This is still new." Words I've heard too many times before. But it feels different this time.

This time it's from Jada.

I kinda get the hang of walking in the skates as we walk to the rink gate. He gets on the ice first, guiding me on and towards the wall. The second my blade touches the ice, my body decides gravity is optional. My legs wobble, like they're completely unsure of what surface they've landed on. The rink feels endless, too bright, too open. My hand snaps to the barrier as if it's a lifeline—and honestly, it kind of is.

Jada would usually already be halfway across the rink, even going slow, he makes it look like he was born on skates. His laughter echos, light and teasing, like a melody I don't deserve to hear but get to anyway. "Come on, Payton! Let go of the wall—you're doing fine!"

"Fine?" I call back, clutching the barrier tighter.

They just grin.

It takes a few minutes—maybe more—but eventually, my legs start remembering how to cooperate. My grip loosens. The cold air brushes my face as I push off, slow at first, then just a little bit faster. It's clumsy, but kind of... freeing. The scrape of the blades, the faint music playing overhead, the sharp scent of the rink—it all blurs into something that almost feels like peace.

Jada glides beside me, cheeks flushed, eyes bright. "See? You're a natural!"

I snort. "Yeah, sure. A natural disaster, maybe."

They laugh—that full, unguarded sound that somehow makes everything in me go still. For a moment, it's just the two of us, suspended in this strange little world of ice and laughter. They smile at me like I'm not something that needs to be fixed. Like I'm someone worth looking at.

And then the doors open.

The sound cuts through everything—the scrape of the hinges, the faint echo of footsteps. I glance toward it, just a reflex, and then I see her.

Viviana.

My stomach drops. The cold isn't just the rink anymore—it's in my chest, my throat, my bones. My whole body locks up before my brain can even catch up. My toe pick catches the ice, there's a sharp jerk, and then I'm falling. The pain hits fast and vicious as my knee collides with the ice. My bad knee. The brace shifts under my jeans, metal digging into my skin.

"Payton!" Jada yelps as I drag them down in my panic. We tumble together in a heap, and they burst into laughter, wiping frost from their hair. "Oh my gosh, that was so bad—it looked like a cartoon fall!"

Their voice is soft and warm, but it feels a mile away. My heart's racing too fast, and I can't catch my breath. The ice beneath me feels like it's melting through my skin.

Why is she here? What does she want? Did she follow me? Did she see us together? What if she—

"Payton."

Jada's voice slices through the noise in my head. I look up, and they're kneeling beside me, eyes full of concern now instead of laughter. "You okay?"

I swallow hard. "Yeah," I lie. My voice shakes anyway. "I think that's all for today though."

They smile, gentle, still trying to read me. "That's fine. We've been here a while anyway."

They help me up, their hand fitting easily into mine. The brace tugs when I stand, a dull ache radiating up my leg, but I pretend not to notice. I always pretend.

We leave the rink slowly, blades clicking against the rubber mats. I can feel Viviana's presence even when I'm not looking, like a shadow crawling under my skin. When we reach the benches, I risk a glance—she's heading into the locker rooms.

Jada sits beside me, pulling off their skates and humming under their breath. "Dinner?" they ask, brushing frost from her sleeve. "I could eat enough fries to fill a small nation."

I laugh—too quickly. "Yeah. Sure. Dinner sounds good."

She doesn't notice how my eyes keep darting toward her bag. When she turns away, I unzip it just enough to check. No note. No folded piece of paper. No sign Viviana's been anywhere near us.

Maybe she didn't see us. Maybe she was just here to skate.

But my hands won't stop shaking as I tie my shoes. The echo of her voice—of what she used to say—plays faintly in the back of my skull.

Maybe she didn't see us.

But I can still feel her eyes on me.

chapter nine

I woke up at 3:00 a.m. again.

Nightmare. Same one, I think. My chest is tight, my shirt clinging with sweat. I try to close my eyes, but every time I blink, the dark turns into a face I don't want to see.

So I get up.

The floor's freezing. I let the shower run too hot, hoping it'll burn the feeling away. By the time I'm out, it's 4:30. I look in the mirror, and for a second, I almost don't recognize myself—the tired eyes, the faint scar peeking out near my jaw, the hollow look that wasn't there before Viviana.

I pull on my clothes, not really caring if they look good, and grab my bag and keys. The apartment feels too small, and yet way too big.

I don't even listen to music as I watch the sun start to rise on my walk to the Bistro. I need something. I don't get to go often on weekdays because of Viviana.

She's always working but not on Thursdays. Which is good, my dad used to bring me all the time when he had his days off. Those were on Thursdays too.

It's still pretty early but I see Vincent behind the counter, setting up the bar for the day.

The bell rings and I hear the faint sound of classical music coming from the back of the store.

"Hey! You're here early." Vincent smirks.

"Couldn't sleep."

"Makes sense. The usual?" he asks.

"Actually..."—the words caught in my throat—"can I get a Hazelnut Cream Latte...with 3 pumps of vanilla?"

Vincent stops wiping the counter. "You sure?"

"Yeah."

"Ok... Switch up, I got you, gimme ten minutes and I'll get started."

I sit at my favorite table. It's not perfect and most of the time people don't like to sit here. The table rocks a bit and some of the coffee rings staining the table just won't budge. It's chipped on the edges, but it's perfect to me. The slight rocking is a nice distraction. Besides, I like to people watch, and it's right by the window.

I'm about to set up my laptop when Vincent puts two drinks down. The Hazelnut Cream I asked for, and my usual matcha.

"What's this..?" I ask, grabbing the matcha.

"Oh please! You act like I don't know you. You're allergic to hazelnuts."

"Then why'd you make it if you know me so well."

"Because I know exactly whose drink this was...and I know what day it is."

I feel my hand grip the cup tighter, disregarding the heat.

"Careful man it's really hot-" he says, reaching over to grab the cup, which I just pull away. "I—" he hesitates, "I'm sorry. I didn't—"

I cut him off with a hand raise. "It's fine."

I watch Vincent out of the corner of my eye, struggling and starting to form the words that I only wanted to hear from my dad before he walked away…saying nothing.

I sit there for hours, pretending I'll get up soon. That I'll open my laptop, maybe start some work, maybe be a functioning person today. But I don't. I can't even bring myself to lift the lid.

My phone buzzes somewhere in my bag, but I don't touch it. I already know what's waiting there—missed calls, messages I don't have the energy to answer.

So I just…sit. Watch the world outside the window keep moving like nothing's wrong. People passing by in pairs, in groups, laughing, rushing somewhere. The sound of conversations drifts around me, light and meaningless. It should make me feel less alone, but it doesn't.

I wonder if anyone out there is having the same kind of day I am—quiet, heavy, and too long to name.

That's when Jada walks in.

They push through the door, looking a tad disheveled. Baggy sweater, ripped jeans, sneakers, and their afro tied back but with only two elastics rather than their usual, I don't know, a million? They usually never look like this.

I watch as they order tea and go to sit down. Jada thanks Vincent as soon as he brings their order, then smacks her head down onto the table as soon as he leaves.

Should I go over there..? I think before cutting myself off, *No I—she probably has enough on her plate...*

I turn away when Jada catches me staring.

"Please, take a picture, it'll last longer."

"I—I'm sorry, I wasn't—I mean, I *was*, but it's not—"

"Relax, calculator watch. I'm kidding..." They smile weakly. "You with someone?" they ask, glancing at the now cold cup of coffee across from him.

"No!" Too fast. "No—I—uh" I clear my throat. Could this be more embarrassing?

"Can I?" They gesture towards the chair.

"Uh—yeah, of course— that would be—sorry. Yes."

They grab her mug and walk over to where I'm sitting. "Someone's on edge today. Something happen?"

"No, sorry, it's just...it's not a good day."

"I get that," she says, slumping down onto the table.

"So—what happened..?"

"It's my stupid physics class!"

I'm a bit taken aback by how angry she gets, I've never seen her like this.

"Every time, every single time, I think I'm getting better! And then, no matter how much I study, every time I fail. I just got my midterm back and it's- it's awful. Even if I win this thing, they'll never let me stay if I keep getting grades like this!" her voice starts to crack as she slumps back to the table once more.

I lean onto my hand, elbow on the edge of the table. "Why don't you try tutoring..?"

"The only tutor the teachers ever recommend is Viviana! With how she treated you? I don't want to be around her."

"Ok, what's between her and I should not impact your grade. I don't care who your tutor is, but you need to be passing your classes..."

"Says the man who skipped today."

"How did you-"

"You don't even have your notebooks with you. Everytime I've seen you here, I never bothered you because you were always doing some kind of homework. Every Thursday, you sit in the same spot and just completely lock in. You don't even notice when Vinny comes around and gives you refills."

She noticed all that just from the past maybe eight weeks..? Not even Viviana knows me that well...

"E-even so...you want this a lot more than I do..." I laugh, very nervously.

"Lightbulb!" she exclaims, "You can tutor me!"

"Wait, what- no- Jada I have two jobs, when would I have time to—"

"You work in the library, right?"

"Well, yes, but that doesn't mean that—"

"And you don't have much to do except reorganize the shelves and that takes like, what, an hour?"

"Yeah, however—"

"So after that you can help me! You'd still be getting paid because you'd be clocked in at the library. It makes perfect sense!" She smiles.

I yell her name, trying to get her attention, and then immediately regret it. I shy away, trying to deflect the attention I drew. "Jada, I don't know. My boss—Janet—uhm—she's nice and all, but she always has something she wants me to do…"

"Maybe I can convince her that this is worthwhile… please?" She begs.

"Ugh…fine. But if I get in trouble, no more."

She nods and grabs my hand. "Thank you!"

I could feel my face heat up, the warmth rushing to my cheeks before I could stop it.

"So- who's the cold coffee for?" she asks, gesturing to the cup once more.

"It's—"

Do I tell her the truth? I should tell her the truth. How do I even do that? How can I even—

"It's for my dad.." I blurt out.

"Did he stand you up?"

"I mean—he—"

"It's alright," he interrupts, "if it helps, my dad's been in jail since I was three."

"Sorry?"

"Yeah, I don't really know much about him. But who needs him? Y'know? I got my moms!"

"What a lore drop...good lord..."

"Sorry." He laughs. "What about yours?"

"I-I don't really—"

"Oh! Sorry, is it sensitive? I get it, it used to be really hard for me to talk about my dad too. I mean, how do you come to terms with the fact that your biological father is a psychopath. It's really hard, people actually pull away because of things like that, but it's not like I made him that way, it's not my fault my dad is a little, ehh, if you know what I mean, like seriously, it's just"—he glances at me—"sorry—I just keep rambling on and on...just know I get it." He sighs.

"N-no it's fine...I don't mind." I huff with a smirk.

He smiles back, a bit embarrassed, and starts to talk about his classes. I feel bad for saying something, but I hate attention...I hate stares, especially. I usually hate when people just talk and talk, but not right now.

*. ❄ * ❄ *. ❄ .* ❄ * ❄ . *

Jada suggests we get out for a while—"clear our heads," they say.

I want to get out of it, to say I wasn't really up for it. But the truth is... I just want to be with them. So I go.

We walk through town in silence for a while. The air has that sharp fall bite to it, cold enough to make my breath visible. The streets are alive—kids dragging parents from store to store, people setting up booths for the Halloween events that start tonight. The smell of pumpkin spice and roasted nuts drifted from somewhere, mixing with the wind.

Jada shoves their hands into their hoodie pockets. "Jeez, it's really cold today—and I even wore my thick hoodie!"

"Here," I say, already slipping off my coat and settling it on their shoulders before they can argue.

They blink, surprised. "You don't have to, really—it's nothing, I'm not that cold, I just—"

"Jada. It's fine."

They give me that look—the one that makes my chest feel too warm for the weather. "It's a nice jacket. Where'd you get it?"

"It was my dad's," I say, glancing down at it. "I think he found it at some thrift store back in the eighties."

"Oh, I love thrifting! Back home we have this place called Thriftable. My siblings and I go there all the time! They take trades, so I get to swap my old clothes for new ones basically for free—it's great!"

I smile a little. "You have siblings?"

"Yeah! Remember? I told you, my brother Tristan and my sister Tia—they're older than me. Twins. I just call him Tris though, everyone does. He usually tags along when I go shopping—mostly to buy new rings or something for his girlfriend, Juliana. She's really sweet." They tilt their head. "Do you have any siblings?"

"Yeah," I say slowly. "I have a brother, Austin. He's sixteen. And... a new little sister, Millie. She's five months now."

Jada's face lit up. "Oh wow, so little!"

"Yeah," I say softly, smiling despite myself. "She's the sweetest. But I'm not really used to babies—it's... hard taking care of her."

"What about your parents?"

"My mom's working again—she's in the maternity ward at IvyMed." I hesitate. "And my dad..."

"Don't tell me he doesn't help!" Jada interrupts, frowning. "Gosh, men today—such jerks, how could a father not—"

"Jada!" The word came out sharper than I meant. My voice cracked halfway through. "He just—he can't, okay?"

Their eyes grow wide. I feel my hands shaking. Shit. Not here. Not now. I turn away and sit down hard on the nearest bench, trying to breathe through it. The air stings my lungs.

Jada follows, quiet now, and sits beside me. "Why not...?"

I swallow hard. The knot in my throat is too thick. "Because he—" The words jam, refusing to move. "Do you remember that accident I told you about a few weeks ago?"

They nod slowly.

I didn't say it. I couldn't. But I didn't have to. I see it in their face when it clicks.

"Oh—oh, oh my gosh, Payton, I didn't know. Why didn't you tell me? I shouldn't have assumed, I just—" They look stricken. "I'm so sorry."

I stare at the ground. "It's... it's okay. I should've said something earlier, but I didn't know how."

"You have nothing to apologize for," they say gently, sliding a hand over my shoulder in a small side hug. Their warmth steadies me a little. After a moment, they look up and point across the street. "How about we take your mind off it?"

I follow their gaze to a shop with a crooked sign that reads Down Thrift Avenue. The display window is cluttered with old denim jackets, faded records, and a disco ball that probably hadn't spun since *Soul Train* was on air.

I manage a faint smile. "Sure."

Jada grins, tugging my sleeve as they stand. And for the first time all day, the air didn't feel quite so heavy.

Inside, the shop smells like old books and fabric softener, a mix of history and something oddly comforting. The shelves are cluttered with everything from vintage jackets to random knick-knacks—porcelain figurines, mismatched teacups, and a collection of postcards from places long forgotten. A faded record player sits in the corner, spinning a soft jazz tune that crackles under the weight of time. The overhead lights flicker slightly, casting a golden glow over the dust motes floating in the air. It feels like stepping into a forgotten story, one where every object has a past waiting to be uncovered.

I watch Jada wander over to the jewelry section, eyes scanning the necklaces. The display case is a jumble of tangled chains, beaded bracelets, and rings that look like they'd been plucked straight out of another era. Some pieces are gaudy, oversized, and flashy, while others are delicate, barely catching the light. They start looking through them all, captivated by how many there are.

I go look at their jackets. I've been meaning to get a new one for Austin. His is starting to tear. Mom also doesn't wear her old winter coat anymore, maybe I can find one here.

I scan the various rows of sweaters, jackets, and coats when I find a light pink coat with a fluffy black rim on the hood. It's her size and it's not too expensive, so she won't kill me over this. I take it with me when I start to search for something for Austin.

He usually just wears my old grey jacket, which doesn't fit either of us anymore. It doesn't help that he wears it when he practices. I know he prefers navy, but he's always in my grey jacket, so I go to the only row of grey they have that's long sleeved. I browse through it and I find a grey letterman jacket. It's got the old Ivywood Early College logo on it.

Perfect.

I grab it and try it on. If it fits me, it's going to fit him.

It looks like it's at least from the 60's, which was the prime time for the Ivywood baseball team. Sad, I know. The stitching looks like it's from the championship games, so they clearly won. It's a nice jacket. Who would give this away?

It doesn't matter, it fits so I'm getting it.

I throw it over my arm with the pink coat and find Jada still in the jewelry section. They're staring at a turquoise crystal with a delicate silver chain.

It isn't anything extravagant, just a simple charm, but they seem entranced by it. The blue-green stone shimmers faintly under the dim lighting, cool and smooth where it rests against the display's velvet lining.

They reach out, brushing their fingers against it, almost testing if it is real.

"That one's nice," the shopkeeper muses from behind the counter, barely glancing up from their book. "Turquoise is for protection, you know. Good luck charm, too." I barely register their words, but Jada strikes up a small conversation with them.

"You like that one?" I ask, beside her as she jumps.

"I didn't see you!" She smiles. "Well, I mentioned I love crystal necklaces and this one is my birthstone."

I raise an eyebrow. "Huh. You didn't tell me that part last time."

"Maybe you need to ask the right questions," she teases. "Nice coat. I didn't think of you as a pink person."

"It's for my mom."

She laughs, then glances at the price tag on the chain.

"You should get it," I say.

She just sighs. "Can't. I don't have the money for it right now."

I didn't say anything else except, "When's your birthday, anyway?"

"December 22nd."

"Cool."

"I'm gonna look at the shoes. Just wanna see what they have." She smiles, and walks away.

I look back towards the necklace and pick it up.

"Are you ready to check out?" the shopkeeper asks.

I nod and follow her to the register.

They put everything into a bag for me and Jada joins me to leave. As soon as we step outside, the wind catches something—then smack. A flyer hits me right in the face. I peel it off, blinking, and Jada bursts into laughter, nearly doubling over.

"Guess the universe really wants you to read that," they tease, plucking the paper from my hand. It's some brightly colored ad for the town's Halloween festival—bonfire, costume contest, late-night skating, the works.

Jada looks at me, eyes still shining with laughter. "Hey...want to go? Halloween night, I mean."

I hesitate for half a second, feeling the leftover warmth from the store still lingering somewhere in my chest. Then I nod. "Yeah. Yeah, I'd like that."

Their smile widens, soft but bright. "Good. It's a date, then."

I try to play it cool, but I can feel my face heating up again. The flyer flutters out of my hand, carried away by the wind.

*. ❄ * ❄ *. ❄ .* ❄ * ❄ .*

It's around eight when I finally get home. The apartment's quiet—too quiet. No sign of Mom, no sign of Austin. Just the sitter.

Then, from the living room, I hear it—Millie's cry. Not just a fussy whimper, but a full-on wail, sharp and desperate, the kind that fills every corner of the room and makes the walls feel smaller.

Ashleigh Little's voice follows soon after, soft but tired. She's sitting on the couch with Millie in her arms, bouncing her gently. Millie's little face is red and scrunched up, her tiny fists clenched, clearly fighting sleep with every ounce of energy she's got.

When Ashleigh sees me, she exhales in relief, like I'm some kind of miracle worker. "Please, you're better at this than I am," she says, laughing softly, and tired, over Millie's hiccuping sobs.

I smile, reaching into my pocket and pulling out the cash I owe her, and a little extra. "Guess she just likes me better."

Ashleigh grins, half-joking, half-exhausted. "If that's the case, she's all yours." She carefully hands Millie over, and the second her tiny body settles against my chest, the crying starts to fade—first to whimpers, then to soft little sniffs. I feel the tension melt out of her. Her fingers clutch at my shirt, her breaths slowing.

Ashleigh shakes her head, smiling in disbelief. "You have a gift, man..."

I laugh quietly. "Or she's just finally tired enough to give up."

"Either way," Ashleigh says, stretching as she stands, "you've got this handled. Night, Payton."

"Night, Ash."

The door closes behind her, leaving me alone with the quiet hum of the apartment and Millie's tiny sighs against my shoulder. I rock her gently, still awkward with the motion, trying to remember the way Dad used to do it.

"Hey, it's okay," I murmur. "You're okay, Millie."

She stirs, a soft cry starting again. I look around the room, searching for something—*anything* —that might help. My eyes land on the record player.

"Alright then... that'll work."

I set The Beatles' Greatest Hits on the turntable and lower the needle. The familiar strum of Golden Slumbers fills the room. I start to sway with her in time to the music, slow and careful. Her cries quiet completely, and by the second verse, she's asleep.

I sit with her on the couch as the rest of the album plays through. The warmth of her tiny body rests against my chest, and for a moment, the world feels still. When the last song ends, I ease her into her crib, careful not to wake her, and put the record away.

On my way to my room, I hear the front door open and a voice—soft, tired. Mom. She's on the phone, whispering something I can't quite make out. I don't bother listening. Instead, I grab two sticky notes and scrawl **"Millie is asleep"** on each, sticking one to her door and one to mine.

I leave my door cracked, just in case Millie wakes up again, and collapse onto my bed. The ceiling stares back at me, blank and familiar. I really don't want to see Mom. It seems like recently, I never really do.

And y'know, I've never been a fan of my birthday.

But today...today was a pretty good day to turn twenty.

chapter ten

Sometimes it's good to procrastinate. Especially when you need some last minute additions to a Halloween costume and you have a bag waiting to go to Goodwill in your living room.

It's mostly things from my closet, but I found my old jean jacket in the bag. I don't wear it anymore so it's still going to the Goodwill or whatever thrift will take it, but I'll give it a good last run with me.

I grew up watching a bunch of 80's and 90's movies with my dad, one of them being *The Breakfast Club*, and I'm hoping Jada did too or she won't understand my costume at all. It's not a perfect costume, but I think it's good enough to pass as John Bender.

"Payton! Austin! Get out here so I can get a picture!" Mom yells from down the hall.

I grab my bag from my desk chair and start down the hall.

"Well, don't you look handsome," Mom says, cupping my face and giving me kisses.

"Mom stop-" I laugh.

"Watch out!" Austin yells. "Here comes the spider-man!!"

He poses at the end of the hall. "Ok small fry, chill."

"Let's hurry this up though, Riley and the group are downstairs!" He smiles, eagerly trying to get me over to the usual picture spot.

"Ok ok, Payton here, hold your sister." Mom hands Millie to me. She is dressed in a little pumpkin costume.

"Ok! Smile!"

I give mom one of those small smiles so she can put that on Facebook.

"Ok one more—"

"Moooooom," Austin whines, "I gotta go!!"

"Alright alright." She walks over to the two of us. "Have a good time with your friends," she kisses Austin on the forehead, then moves over to me, taking Millie and giving me a kiss on the cheek. "Have a good time with Jada, I'll call you if I need you."

"Ok, we'll see you—"

"You both gotta call me if anything changes, keep your locations on. Ok?"

"Ok!" we say in unison. "Bye mom!" Austin yells, running out the door.

"Don't worry, we'll be fine," I say, giving her a smile before closing the door.

Austin and I get in the elevator. "Don't be stupid."

"I won't."

"I'm serious, is your phone charged?"

"Yes." He sighs.

"Do you have a portable charger?"

"Yep."

"What's my phone number?"

"… 768-9353," he mumbles. "Payton, I'll be fine. You're being paran—" he cuts himself off, as I shoot him a look.

"I just want you to be careful. Ok?"

"And I'm saying I will be. Just trust me. I'll call you if I need you, ok?" Austin pushes.

"Fine…Have fun," I say as the elevator doors open.

Austin joins his friends and I walk with him and his group to town.

We haven't even gone far before someone tosses out a casual, "We should've just taken the car."

They laugh it off a second later, already moving on, but the words hook into me and refuse to let go.

I keep replaying them as we walk—slowly, because of me.

Because of my leg.

Because everything takes longer now.

Maybe they're right.

Maybe I am holding everyone up.

Maybe I should've stayed home.

Maybe—

"Payton!"

My name pulls me out of my head. I look up and see Jada waving from a bench, practically bouncing like they've been waiting forever. Their smile is so bright it knocks the wind out of whatever dark place I was sliding into.

I walk over, and before I can even say anything, they grab my sleeve.

"There you are! C'mon, you have to see what they set up on Main Street."

I barely get out a "hello" before they're already leading me towards the music and lights.

We end up spending the next few hours just... wandering. It's the kind of night that doesn't try too hard to be perfect but ends up getting close anyway.

A band is playing on a small stage, and when they start a song Jada loves, they nudge me.

"Oh, we're dancing. No backing out."

"I don't dance," I say, already getting pulled forward.

"You're with me, therefore you dance. That's the rule."

It's stupid and chaotic and we are absolutely off-beat, but somehow it works. We stumble and laugh and almost fall when Jada attempts some dramatic spin I absolutely cannot help them pull off, but it's fun. Simple, loud, warm fun.

Then we hit the booth section.

"Ring toss?" Jada asks, eyebrows raised.

"I will lose," I say.

"That's the spirit, sorta!"

They win a tiny stuffed bat on their second try and immediately place it on my shoulder.

"There. It suits you."

"It's cross-eyed."

"You have glasses, potato-potahto." She laughs.

We walk more, letting the crowd move around us. The air smells like cinnamon and kettle corn, and someone's blasting a Halloween playlist loud enough to rattle the streetlights.

Eventually, we find a mocktail booth lit up with purple LED lights. The guy running it is dressed as a zombie doctor.

"What can I get for you two?" he asks.

"Something fruity?" I say.

"Something that looks like it could power a spaceship," Jada adds.

He hands me a strawberry drink and Jada something neon blue that sparkles.

"Oh my god," she says, staring into the cup. "If this stains my tongue, I'm suing."

"You can't sue a man in zombie makeup," I say.

"I can, and I will." She grins, nudging my arm.

We keep walking, sipping our drinks. Mine actually tastes good. Jada's keeps leaving glitter on her lip, which they insist is "for the aesthetic."

For a while, I forget everything—my leg, the comments earlier, the heavy stuff waiting at home. It's just us weaving through the festival, talking about absolute nonsense and pretending we're way better at carnival games than we are.

By the time the sky is fully dark, it feels like the night stretched itself just for us.

Then my phone buzzes in my pocket—once, then again, then a third time. Persistent.

I almost ignore it, but the vibration keeps going, steady and insistent, tugging at the edges of the moment. I pull it out, look at the screen—it's Mom.

I sigh. "Sorry—it's my mom. Gimme a sec," I say, motioning to my phone before moving out of the way of the street so I can hear her.

"Hey, what's up?" I start to say before I'm cut off.

"What's taking you so long!" she yells, "The hospital called, one of my patients needs me. I need you home now."

"OK—but why are you calling me and not Ashleigh?"

"She didn't pick up."

"Mom, you said I'd be fine to stay out til 12 when your shift started."

"No," she emphasizes, "I said Austin could, I said I'd call you if something changes."

"Mom, that's not fair, why do I have to—"

"I need you home within the next 30 minutes. Leave now."

"But—"

"Now." She hangs up.

"Whatever..." I whisper, shoving my phone into my pocket. "Jada, I'm sorry—I have to go home. My mom needs me to babysit."

"Oh... it's alright..." She looks more upset than I thought she'd be. I wanna say something but—no, it's dumb. I start to walk away as Jada says, "Maybe I can walk you home?"

"Oh—you don't have to, it's Ok—" I cut myself off.

She still wants to hang out with me..?

"I mean- yeah- I'd like that..."

She lights up, nearly skipping to join me on my walk home. I fall into step beside her, still carrying that warm buzz from the festival—even if my feet are starting to hate me.

We talk about practice on the way, mostly Jada rambling about what she should go over next time.

"We should definitely work on edge control," she says, hands flying everywhere as usual.

"Oh—and the crossovers. You should join me! You're getting better on the ice, I swear, but we can tighten them up."

"You're acting like you're my coach," I say, nudging them lightly with my shoulder.

"I basically am," she shoots back. "Just. I don't know...when we both have time. Y'know. Soon."

I roll my eyes. "Jada, I almost took both of us out last time."

"Yeah, but in a cute way."

"I don't think concussions come in *cute*."

He laughs, brushing me off. "So that's a yes?"

I don't want to disappoint him—not after tonight—so I give him a softer, more honest answer. "Maybe."

It seems to be enough. He grins and keeps talking, weaving between people on the sidewalk. The crowd's still out for the Halloween events, so it's a lot of dodging costumes, candy bags, and three-foot-tall witches.

Then Jada bumps into someone—hard enough to make him stumble.

"Oh my gosh—sorry, I didn't—"

He stops when she sees who it is as I help him regain his balance again.

Some girl, tall, pretty, covered in pink.

And Viviana, standing close beside her.

My stomach drops.

Before Jada can finish apologizing, Viviana steps between them. "Back off."

The girl touches her arm quickly. "Viv—hey, I'm fine."

"They should be watching where they're going," Viviana says, eyes sharp.

"Viv, seriously." The girl then moves her aside with a gentle push, offering Jada an apologetic look. "I'm so sorry about her."

"No, it's okay," Jada says quickly. "She's right—I should've been paying attention. I'm sorry."

"Don't even worry about it," she says. "Same for me. I'm Esme."

"Jada," he replies. Then they gesture toward me. "And this is Payton."

My eyes widen a little. I'm already shaking my head behind Jada's back, making a small cut it out motion. *Why me? Why now?*

Esme's eyes land on me—and I watch recognition wash over her face.

Ah. Great.

Perfect.

Viviana notices too. She steps forward, fingers gently curling around Esme's hand. "We should go," she mutters, not quite looking at me.

Esme hesitates only a second. "It—it was nice meeting you both."

They turn and head down the sidewalk. I stay frozen for a moment, watching them disappear into the crowd. Viviana glances back once, right before they turn a corner—her eyes meeting mine for half a second.

I look away fast. Too fast.

"Let's go," Jada murmurs.

But I'm looking back, staring at where Viviana vanished, the echo of her look lingering.

She didn't have the same hatred in her eyes as before.

And somehow, that scares me more.

*. ❄ * ❄ *. ❄ .* ❄ * ❄ .*

We get to my apartment building, and stop at the curb. As Jada's about to say goodbye—this soft, warm 'I had a nice time' kind of goodbye—I feel this pit open in my stomach.

I don't want the night to end. Not yet.

Not with her standing right there looking like she might actually mean the "nice time" part.

"Wait—!"

She turns a little too quick. "Yes?"

"Do you—uh—wanna come up?"

She pauses, slower this time. "I'd love to."

That smile of hers hits me right in the ribs.

We get in the elevator. It's quiet for a second before she snorts, telling me about the kid she saw who showed up dressed like Miguel O'Hara from *Spiderman* and walked into a trash can. I laugh harder than I should, mostly because I'm nervous and she's right there next to me. When the doors open, she follows me out.

The moment I unlock the apartment, my mom comes flying past like she's late for literally everything.

"Hi, hun—sorry! Food's in the fridge and—who's this?"

"Hi, I'm Jada," she says.

"Oh, so you're the one Payton won't stop talking about."

"Mom—!" I grit my teeth. "Don't you have somewhere to be?"

"I'm going! Nice to meet you, Jada!"

She practically launches herself into the elevator.

I exhale. "Sorry about that. Uh, come in."

I head to my mom's room to check on Millie—she's asleep, sprawled out like she owns the place. Jada's right behind me in the hall, looking around like they're trying not to stare too much.

"I like your apartment," they say.

"Thanks. My dad designed it."

"Oh—was he, like, an interior designer?"

"Construction worker." I shrug. "He designed the building."

"That's really cool."

They look toward my door. "Is that your room?"

"Yeah—uh, just gimme a sec."

I slip inside and immediately go into panic mode: clothes off the floor and stuffed into any drawer that'll close, bed straightened, vinyl covers stacked so they at least pretend to have a system. I check the room like three times before opening the door again.

"Okay. You can come in."

She wanders in, eyes wide, taking everything in. "Your room's awesome. Oh—I love this one." She stops in front of the biggest poster. "NASA?"

"Yeah. I wanted to work there."

"Seriously?"

"Had a whole plan and everything."

"So...what happened?"

I swallow. "It just...didn't work out. Back then."

She steps closer and puts a hand on my shoulder. It's gentle, and somehow that makes it worse. "Maybe you can make it work now."

"...Maybe."

Jada clears their throat and gestures toward the corner of my room.

"So—you play?"

I shrug. "Yeah. Since I quit soccer. Needed something to do."

They step closer, tapping one of the drums. "Teach me."

I snort before I can stop myself. "You? On drums?"

They grin like they've already won. "What, you don't think I can?"

"Absolutely not."

"Rude."

"I'm just being honest."

They huff and move toward the set like they're about to prove something. It's adorable.

They pick up the sticks, throw me one nervous glance, then attempt... whatever that beat was supposed to be.

I can't help it, I'm laughing. "You're awful."

Their face falls. "I'm trying!"

They are. Just... very badly. I shake my head, still smiling. "Come on. Scoot over."

They roll their eyes but shift to the side, leaving just enough room for me to slide onto the seat beside them. We're close. My brain short-circuits for a second.

Before they can notice, I reach out and cover their hands with mine, adjusting their grip on the sticks. Their fingers are warm. Mine are definitely shaking.

"Relax," I murmur. "You're overthinking it."

"I am not—"

"You are." I nudge their hands gently into place. "Just follow my lead, yeah?"

They swallow. Nod.

I tap out a simple rhythm, guiding their hands with mine. At first their movements are choppy, hesitant, but slowly they start falling into the beat. The bass drum thuds steady beneath my foot, the snare cracks sharp and clean under our hands.

They're still tense, but that spark of excitement starts leaking through.

I lean in a little without meaning to, my voice brushing their ear.

"See? You're a natural."

They scoff, breathless. "That's probably cheating, though."

Maybe it is.

But I don't move my hands away.

She's still catching her breath when she nudges me lightly with her shoulder.

"Okay," she says, trying for casual and missing by a mile, "now you have to play something. Like... actually play. For real."

I blink. "For you?"

She shrugs, but her ears turn pink. "If you want."

I try not to smile too hard and fail immediately. "Yeah...ok."

I spin the sticks in my fingers, settle my feet, and launch into a short, clean groove — nothing flashy, just something warm and steady that fills the room without swallowing her quiet wonder. When I finish, she's staring at me like I've just performed a magic trick.

"That was..." Her voice dips, soft and honest. "Really good."

My heart does a weird leap-and-stumble thing.

Jada lets out a low breath, almost a laugh. "You could really do something with this...Join a band or something."

I shake my head, but the compliment hits harder than any snare crack. "Maybe," I say, trying not to sound as hopelessly flattered as I feel.

She turns a little, and then her eyes go ridiculously wide. "Are those—do you have bunnies?!"

"Oh—yeah." I can't help smiling. "Jada, meet Tofu and Mochi."

"They're adorable."

"Mochi's shy. She's probably hiding. Wanna hold one?"

She looks offended I even asked. "Yes. Obviously."

I laugh, open their crate, and lift Mochi from her usual hiding spot in the back.

"Here—careful."

Jada holds her like she's a rare treasure or something. "Look at her," she whispers. Then she looks down at her own arm, then at Mochi. "Oh my god—we have matching spots. We're basically twins."

I'm supposed to be watching the bunny, but honestly? I'm watching her.

Before I can stop myself, I pull out my phone.

"Smile," I say quietly.

She looks up, grins—really grins—and I take the picture.

chapter eleven

"Let's run it one more time," I yell to Jada as she glides on the ice. "Just for good measure!"

I see her smile back at me, giving me a thumbs up.

She's doing an amazing job. Jada runs through the routine one last time, and I swear I'm trying to play it cool, but I'm basically staring like an idiot. Everything she does is sharp and clean, the kind of thing that makes you forget to blink. I'm proud of her—stupidly proud—but no way am I saying that out loud. Not yet. I'll never hear the end of it.

When she gets to the axel, she switches it out for the double we've been using to build up to the triple. And she nails it. Perfect takeoff, perfect landing.

She comes to a stop, breathing hard, brushing hair out of her face, and all I can think is: she needs a break. She's doing great, but she won't progress if she's tired.

"That was great! I think that's a good stopping point for today," I say, ready to go.

"Are you kidding? I'm on a roll, can I at least try the triple?"

"I don't think that's a good idea- we haven't walked through it yet..."

"Oh come on, Payt, lemme live a little."

"I am, by keeping you from doing this. So you won't die, like you said before."

"Haha hilarious."

I stare at her, deadpan.

"Please," she begs. "Just once or twice then we can be done."

I keep the stare up as she looks me in the eyes... curse her stupid look. I break. "Fine...Just once."

She stimms happily and starts the routine again.

It starts off fine as she works her way up the jump, each twist and turn going just fine. When she reaches the jump it looks like she was actually going to do it, but she takes off wrong and I can see the look on her face shift from confidence to fear. She lands on her knee and slides with her head hitting the ground.

"JADA—!" I yell, running into the ice.

I help him sit up as he checks himself for bruises. I notice the blood on his knee and the new cut on his forehead.

"I-I'm fine. I'm good."

I take a shaky breath, trying to look calm even though my chest is tight.

I help them up without saying anything, one hand under their arm, the other steadying their elbow. They're laughing it off—of course they are.

"Clearly, we still have work to do—"

I ignore that and check the cut on their forehead. It isn't deep, but to me it looks awful all the same.

"I think maybe next time I'll start with just trying the jump, working up to it and stuff," Jada keeps rambling as I walk off. I grab the first aid kit from the wall and come back. "But I think I'll have it by tryouts. What do you think?"

They finally notice what I'm doing.

"I think... you should've listened to me," I mutter.

"All that for a cut?"

"It could get infected," I say quietly, a little sharper than I meant. I clean the cut, Jada hissing when the disinfectant hits.

"Payton, it's fine, seriously. I've had worse."

"It could've been worse," I snap before I can stop myself. "You're lucky it's just this! What if you hit your knee and dislocated it?" I bandage their knee, hands shaking. "What if you landed wrong and broke your foot?"

"Yeah, but I didn't—"

"But you could've!"

The last word comes out cracked. My voice trembles. I feel it happening before I can stop it.

"You're too reckless and you could—you could get hurt. Badly. And—"

My breath bails on me. "And—uhm—"

"Payt...?" Jada's voice softens.

I shake my head and get up too fast, stumbling toward the back of the bleachers. I slide down the wall, pressing my palms against the floor like that would keep me from falling further. My vision blurs at the edges, and everything feels too loud and too close.

All this because Jada got hurt? Seriously? What the *hell* is wrong with me?

I just want to go home. I want it to stop.

"P--t-n!" Their voice breaks through the ringing in my ears—muffled but there. They kneel in front of me, taking my hands gently.

He runs his thumb over my knuckles, in slow circles. "What's your name?"

I blink. "W-what?"

"Your name. Tell me."

"P-payton. Payton Itsuki Lee."

"How old are you?"

"Twenty..." My vision starts to refocus, shapes returning.

"Where are you right now?"

"We're... we're at the rink. Rink 2. Behind the bleachers."

My breathing finally begins to even out.

He exhales, relieved. "Breathe with me, ok?

I just nod, unable to say anything else. In for four, hold for five, out for six.

"Feel better?"

"A little," I say.

He nods, rambling again—nervous. "I mean, obviously you don't feel good-good, I know panic attacks feel like crap, so I meant feeling less crappy, not like—"

"Yeah," I cut in. It comes out soft.

He blinks, surprised, then sits cross-legged in front of me. "What happened?"

I stare at the scuffed floor. How am I supposed to explain it? That trauma still crawls up my spine anytime someone *I cared about* gets hurt?

"I... don't really know," I lie. "They just... happen sometimes."

"I get that," he says gently.

We sit in silence for a minute. It feels... okay.

"I'll be more careful. I'm sorry," she says.

"No—don't. Don't do that. You didn't do anything wrong. I didn't trust you, and I— I know I'm overly cautious—"

"Payton," she interrupts. "Just let me apologize."

I look up, startled.

"I'm reckless. You're right. And I knew it might freak you out and I still did it. I shouldn't have ignored you. I'm sorry."

Her eyes are steady on mine.

"It's... it's okay," I tell her.

She helps me up, letting me lean on her until my balance comes back. We walk to the front of the bleachers and sit down again. I grab a bandage and gently place it on her forehead.

"There," I say.

"Now I'm perfect." She grins. "You look like you could use a cinnamon roll. Bistro?"

"Yeah... sure." I can't help smiling.

chapter twelve

When I opened my eyes, *I was back in the bathroom, sitting against the cold tile of the shower wall, and for a moment, I couldn't remember how I got there—hadn't I just been in my room?.*

The memory dissolved the second I reached for it, and everything felt heavy, like my bones were filled with cement and my muscles were only guessing how to move.

I pushed myself to my feet, though every limb dragged behind the command, and I limped toward the door, each step a violent argument between gravity and pain—my leg was on fire, screaming with each movement, a voice beneath my skin pleading with me to fall, just fall, give up and sink.

I grabbed the doorknob—it turned—and I pulled, but it wouldn't budge, like the door had fused shut in the time it took to blink. I yanked again, then again, with every ounce of strength until something gave way and I stumbled back, the knob still clutched in my hand like a broken trophy. But when I looked up, the door was whole again—no hole, no knob, not even a scratch from where it would've been—just smooth wood and still air that tasted stale.

I slammed my fists against it, pain blooming in my knuckles, and the sound came back to me warped and distant like I was shouting underwater.

Then I heard whispering—soft, layered voices from nowhere and everywhere—and I turned toward the mirror, and there I was.

Except it wasn't me.

I had my face, kind of, but younger—no facial hair, longer hair, shorter...Everything was different.

I stepped closer.

The mirror did too.

I reached out.

It matched me.

But then its hand reached through and grabbed me—ice-cold fingers around my wrist—and the shower behind me burst on, loud and aggressive, water gushing with unnatural speed, pooling on the floor, rising up my calves, my waist, my chest within seconds.

My breath stuttered.

The mirror held tight.

I kicked at the glass to break free, and that's when more hands reached through—gray and human and yet not human at all—yanking me forward as I gasped one last breath, trying to scream, trying to do something as the bathroom flooded completely, and I was pulled through.

Then I was falling.

Just falling, weightless in the dark, with no idea where the ground was, until I crashed through something sharp—glass?—and landed hard in a tiny, familiar space: the science lab closet from high school.

My arm was bleeding, I was dizzy, and every breath was a struggle.

I stumbled forward, peering through the vent slit, and there she was—Viviana, crying, just like...that day.

My chest ached. I remembered the rage, the betrayal, the way everything shattered. I pushed the door open—and time warped again.

The lab was the same, but the moment had shifted.

We stood in the same place, just months later. She was still crying, but now there was heat behind it, fury barely held back.

I watched us fight. I watched her involuntarily raise her hand. I watched how scared she looked afterward, like she didn't recognize herself either.

And I left her then, didn't I?

I didn't look back. I just wanted to be anywhere else. I opened the door slightly.

Then the Viviana in the room—the real one—turned and saw me, like she'd known I was watching.

Her eyes lit up with something bright and terrifying, and she rushed at me, shoving me with impossible strength back through the closet door—and suddenly I was in the middle of a street.

Cars tore past me, honking, shrieking, metal blurs just inches away. I ran, or tried to, dodging them until I landed in a lane with nothing coming.

I looked up. Stillness in the street turned into an intersection. And then—headlights. A truck. Hurtling toward me.

The horn shattered the silence. I turned again, and there it was—my car. I was behind the wheel.

Alone?

I looked at myself and the me in the driver's seat stared back with eyes like stone and mouthed something before slamming on the gas, veering past me, and getting obliterated by the truck.

The crash knocked me off my feet and sent me tumbling down a hill, skidding toward a lake. I couldn't move—my leg throbbed like it was filled with nails—and I tried to crawl, to breathe, anything.

Then he appeared.

My dad.

Standing calm at the edge of the water, holding out his hand. I took it, breath catching in my throat, but when I leaned into him for safety he pulled me close and whispered, "This is all your fault," and shoved me straight into the lake.

I couldn't scream. I couldn't fight. I just sank.

Faster than I should've, deeper than I should've, darkness wrapping around me like arms I couldn't escape, and the pressure in my chest built until there was nothing but water, and fear, and silence.

I jolt awake, gasping, soaking in sweat, tears already halfway down my face.

My arm stings—I look down and see blood. Real. Still warm.

I pinch myself.

I'm awake.

I have to be.

I wrap it in a bandage with shaking hands, throw on a sweater, and leave my room, needing air, needing silence. But the apartment isn't silent. The TV is still on in the living room, some late-night infomercial droning in the background, light flickering across the wall.

I step closer and find Mom there, passed out on the couch, her head tilted back, mouth slightly open, exhaustion carved into every line of her face. And curled up against her chest, small fingers tucked against her chin, is Millie. Asleep with her socks halfway off and no blanket, one tiny arm dangling dangerously close to the edge of the couch. I freeze, the anger rising before I can stop it. She is asleep. They are asleep. Just like that. No baby monitor, no light left on, just the two of them crumpled into each other like a sad portrait.

I know she's tired. God, I know she's tired. But that doesn't mean she gets to stop being a mother. Not when it matters.

Not when Millie could've rolled off and hit her head.

Not when I'm the one waking up from nightmares and still somehow being the parent. I walk over and gently pick up Millie, adjust her sock, and take her to her crib, placing a blanket over her tiny frame. I walk back over to Mom and pull the throw blanket off the top of the couch and tuck it over her, swallowing the lump in my throat.

I stand there for a moment, staring at them both, feeling that tightness return to my chest—not grief, not exactly. Something heavier.

This isn't how it's supposed to be.

I'm twenty. Twenty. And I've spent the last few years raising Austin like *I'm* the one who had him. Like *I'm* the one who's supposed to give up everything to keep the rest of this house from collapsing.

Mom and Dad were always busy with work. Then Dad died and Mom added someone new to the mix.

And it's not fair.

It's not fair that I don't get to choose. It's not fair that no one looks after *me*.

I back away slowly, making sure they were both okay, then slip out the door as quietly as I can. I climb up to the roof and sit there under the stars, just staring, wondering if they'd disappear the second I believe in them.

chapter thirteen

As much as mom protests, she isn't winning this one.

I need to not be in the house for a bit and a walk is the way to do that.

It's been my escape for a few nights, actually. The holiday lights are starting to go up around town. I'm not sure why. I mean, Thanksgiving is in two weeks, why can't they wait?

I walk past the bistro, seeing their usual plants switched out for Christmas garlands with warm white lights.

That's when someone slams into my shoulder hard enough to spin me half a step. A girl, speed-walking toward the crosswalk with her hood half up. Her bag hits the pavement, papers scattering, and she freezes for a second before looking up at me with wide eyes.

"Sorry—! I'm so sorry," she blurts.

I know who she is immediately.

"Shit—are you okay?" I ask, already crouching beside her, gathering loose pens and a notebook that had flipped open. I hold it out to her, keeping my voice low. "Here—got it."

"Yes! Sorry—I—I'm so sorry. I'm such a scatter-brain today."

I stand back up, extending a hand, "You're-Esme? right?"

"Oh-yeah. How did you-?"

"I'm Payton—"

She tenses. "Oh..! Vivi's—"

"Yeah." There's a moment of awkward silence.

"Why are you in such a rush anyways?" I ask, flicking a leaf off her shoulder.

"I—missed my bus. Viv has the car today and I live across town. I wanted to try getting back before dark and I lost track of time and Viv is working..."

"Do you have anyone to come get you?"

"No one that won't take an hour to get here…" She laughs weakly.

I hesitate. *Am I really about to ask this?* "Out of the blue here, but do you want someone to walk you home?"

"I don't want to be a bother, it's fine- I can try to call my baba—"

"It's really no problem, I'm not doing anything else," I interrupt *God, I sound like such a creep*!

"I mean— that would be great…are you sure? I'm all the way across town. Like forty-five minutes walking…"

"I don't mind." I smile, relieved she didn't think I'm insane. I honestly want to get my mind off things, maybe this could be a good distraction.

She thanks me and we start walking.

While we walk, we end up talking about… pretty much anything. Nothing too heavy. Just whatever comes up.

At one point, Esme glances over at me and says, "Y'know, you're not what I thought you'd be like."

"Really?" I raise a brow.

"Yeah." She laughs a little, tugging her jacket tighter.

"What did you imagine?"

"I dunno— I guess, and please don't take this as an insult, a jerk...?"

I shove my hands deep into my pockets and let out a humorless scoff. "Honestly, that doesn't surprise me."

"Really?"

"Viviana hates me. I really shouldn't expect anything else."

"That's the thing though," she says, slowing a bit. "Why?"

"Why what?"

"Why do you think she hates you?"

I almost trip over a crack in the sidewalk. "I don't think it. I know it."

"How do you know?" she presses gently. "Anytime she sees you she just gets sad. Not... angry."

"I'm surprised she didn't tell you," I mutter.

"Well, she doesn't really talk about high school. And I didn't go to Sierra."

"But you live in the area—? Where'd you go?"

"Sycamore Hill."

"Damn, Blue Jays? We hated you guys." I snort.

"Right back at ya." She laughs, bumping her shoulder lightly against mine.

"Honestly though, it surprises me."

"How so?" she asks.

"I mean, all she did was talk about the 'shitty' things I did after we broke up," I say with a sigh. "I'm surprised she didn't do the same to you." She gets quiet. *Shit.* That was stupid, why did I say that—"Sorry," I add quickly. "I shouldn't be—like—bad-mouthing her like that. I know y'all are dating."

"No, it's—I get it," she says. "But the girl *I'm* with? She's *not* your ex."

That throws me. I look at her, confused.

"From the way you've talked about her, versus how I know her," she goes on. "Those are two different people."

I scoff. "Yeah—right."

"What, you don't think people can change?"

"I do—"

"Then what's the problem?" she shoots back, interrupting me.

"It—It's complicated," I say, staring ahead. "And you don't know what I know..."

She pauses, then gives me this small, almost stubbornly kind smile. "Alright. Touchè."

We keep walking, side by side.

And I'm not mad at her. Even if I want to be, I don't think I could manage it.

She's weirdly easy to talk to.

Yeah, she pushed a bit, but not in a way that makes me want to leave.

It's...nice.

And she doesn't pry, it's like she could tell what I could handle.

Honestly? I kinda like having her here.

We keep walking until we get to this small apartment complex, completely lit, with a playground in the middle, and a lot of pastels.

"This is me!" She smiles.

I glance around a bit and see some families, some couples, some people just sitting on benches. It seems fitting that Esme lives here.

"Thanks for walking me back, I really appreciate it."

"Oh yeah, of course."

She turns to walk away, before pausing and turning around again.

"Can I see your phone for a sec?"

"Um-sure?" I question, skeptical but ok with it as I opened my phone.

She goes into my contacts and starts typing. "Y'know- if you ever wanna hang out or," she takes a picture, "talk about anything, I'm here."

She hands my phone back before walking happily into her complex and disappearing from view.

I just watch as she leaves before looking down at my phone.

Seeing the contact, it's real...*I'm never gonna actually call her*...I think as I go to hit the delete contact button. I want nothing to do with someone who has Viviana as a constant in their lives...but, I feel myself hesitate. My thumb then moves to the exit button, keeping her contact. I plug in my earbuds and start walking back home.

chapter fourteen

Alec Benjamin echoes in my earbuds, Jada humming along with the song she picked.

We share my earbuds as we walk down the street together to the bistro, the wind pushing against us.

I could see the crowd from where we are and I know Jada notices too as we weave through the clusters of people, the smell of kettle corn drifting through the air. Jada's eyes light up when she spots what the crowd surrounds—street performers juggling fire under a halo of early evening lights.

Before I could ask what she is looking at, she grabs my hand and tugs me toward them.

And God—that *shock* goes straight up my spine.

Not because she'd pulled me.

But because she doesn't let go.

Her hand stays in mine, warm and sure, like she'd done it a hundred times before. Like this is normal.

We wander past the performers—down the slope of Main Street, past store windows filled with premature holiday decorations—and she still doesn't let go. I keep waiting for that moment, the drop, the release, the casual "oops, sorry." But nothing.

Just her fingers curling gently around mine, swinging slightly as she walks.

I feel my pulse tripping over itself. I'm fighting every urge in my body not to turn seventeen shades of red. Because it doesn't feel like a "friend grip". Not even close. It feels...intentional.

And I—

I don't pull away.

If anything, I realize I'd adjusted my hold a little, without thinking. Rebalanced. Like my hand wanted to fit better around hers, even though my brain is screaming for backup.

I'm not used to this.

But I settle into it so easily it scares the hell out of me.

I keep my guard up—of course I did, I always do—but the edges are starting to thaw. Not melt, not yet. More like a crack running across a frozen lake, thin and hesitant, but undeniable.

We keep walking, hand in hand, like it's the most natural thing in the world.

When we finally get to the bistro, we're actually more excited to go in than before.

But, as I grab the handle to let Jada in, I see Viviana working, through the window. I swear my brain stutters, my hand misses the handle and I hit my wrist.

"What's goin' on-? You ok?" Jada asks, letting my other hand go, which somehow makes this whole brain glitch worse.

She looks inside and sees Viviana. "Here, I'll go get the coffee. You wait out here."

"No it's fine—" I try to say as Jada gives me a look. Apparently, it is clearly not fine.

Sure, I'm uncomfortable...but it surprises me whenever Jada could see it better than anyone had been able to in years.

How does she do that?

"Fine—" I sigh, "But I'm paying."

"Not if I don't let you!" She pushes past, laughing, and runs in without taking my card.

*. ❄ * ❄ *. ❄ .* ❄ * ❄ .*

We cut across the park, the air colder now, the sky dimming into that early-winter blue. Our coffees are warm against our palms, and—yeah—our hands somehow find each other again. No dramatic moment, no announcement. Just...there.

But Jada keeps glancing at me. Quiet. Too quiet for her.

I catch her fidgeting with one of my bracelets—twisting it, stopping, twisting again.

"Hey, what's up?" I ask.

"Nothing—!" she says, way too fast.

"Oh please," I say, raising a brow, "I can literally feel you rearranging my jewelry."

"It's seriously fine."

"If something's bothering you, you can tell me." I guide her toward a bench, setting my coffee on the armrest. "I'm not gonna bite."

She bites her lip, clearly battling herself. "I don't want you to be upset—it doesn't mean anything, I swear—"

"Just tell me," I say, a little hurt she thought I'd blow up on her.

And if only I knew what was coming.

They aren't wrong to tread carefully. Viviana isn't exactly a story I unpacked for fun. I didn't even tell my mom. All she ever got was: We don't talk anymore. Don't ask.

So when Jada finally blurts, "It's just—she makes you all... eugh—y'know, and I hate seeing you like that." They wince like they expect me to bolt.

But I don't.

"It's okay," I say quietly. "I get why you're curious." A beat. "It's... a really long story."

They scoot closer—way closer—like she's settling in for a movie. I huff out a laugh.

"We'd known each other since fifth grade," I begin. "She was my best friend for, like...six years."

"Yeah?"

"Yeah. We did everything together...then we started dating."

"Oh." Her eyes widened. "Oh—!"

"Yeah," I say dryly. "I didn't know much about her home life—and that's not my business to share—but it messed with us. Messed with her. And eventually...ruined everything."

Jada's expression softens. "Payt..."

"We broke up after—she did something. And a few months later, there was some stupid miscommunication. She got mad. Things were said—" I swallow. "Actions were taken. And we haven't spoken since."

"Jeez, Payton...I'm sorry. That sucks."

I shrug, staring down at my coffee like it holds the secrets of the universe. "Yeah. But it's whatever."

"Sorry I brought it up."

"No—it's okay." I nudge her shoulder. "With how often we keep running into her, you had every right to ask."

She hesitates, then gently places her hand over mine. Warm. Steady.

"Well hey," she says, smiling up at me, "you've got me now. And I don't plan on going anywhere."

I'm not gonna lie, I actually believed her when she said that.

I squeeze her hand, a small smile tugging at my mouth. "Good," I say lightly. "Because you still need tutoring, remember? You're stuck with me until you actually somewhat understand physics."

She groans dramatically, leaning her head against my shoulder.

"Ugh, right. My *favorite* part of our friendship."

"Hey," I say, laughing, "I make those sessions fun."

She nudges me. "Only because you bring snacks."

"Snacks count as educational tools."

And for a moment, the cold doesn't feel so cold. The park doesn't feel so empty.

Because she is here.

And she isn't planning on going anywhere.

*. ❄ * ❅ *. ❆ .* ❅ * ❄ .*

Later that night, after walking Jada back to her campus, I go to the bistro alone, earbuds in, letting my rock playlist keep my brain from chewing itself apart while I hammer out the last paragraphs of my final paper. By the time I hit "save," my coffee was long gone—just a ceramic mug sitting abandoned on the table like a crime scene.

Out of the corner of my eye, I see a hand reach for it.

I look up—and flinch before I could stop myself.

Viviana.

"Jeez—chill out," she mutters, rolling her eyes. "I'm just cleaning up."

I don't say anything. Didn't need to. I didn't even know she was here. She grabs the mug, walks away, and I could practically feel the old tension clinging to my skin like smoke.

Minutes pass. The bistro slowly empties out. Chairs scrape. Conversations fade. Lights dim. And eventually...it's just me and her.

Perfect.

I start to pack my things, shoving my laptop into my bag as she walks by again to grab the last mug on my table.

"Payton—" she says.

I freeze. Just for a second. Then turn halfway—only enough to glance at her over my shoulder.

"Look—I just…" She takes a breath. "We can't keep doing this."

"Sure we can." I say.

She scoffs under her breath. "Seriously—Payt, it's been years."

I swing my bag over my shoulder. "And somehow, I'm still dealing with it."

"Payton," she says, voice tight, "I know things ended badly, but—we can't hold onto this anymore."

I laugh. Actually laugh. "Right. You blamed me for something that wasn't even my fault, hurt me, and never spoke to me again. Hell, you didn't even have the right to be mad about it after what you did to me."

"You don't even know the half of what I went through at the time—"

"And I don't want to."

My voice cracks through the empty café, sharp enough to startle both of us. "I know enough and it doesn't excuse what you did."

The espresso machine hums low in the corner. A streetlamp outside flickers against the icy window.

Silence holds for a moment.

Then, softer: "Y'know..." Viviana murmurs. "I'm different now."

I stare at her. Not angry—just tired.

"Good for you."

"You could at least try to believe me."

That makes me turn fully. Slowly. She searches my face for anything—anger, pity, softness—but I kept it blank. Unreadable.

"Payt..." she whispers.

"You don't get to call me that."

Her mouth opens, but no sound comes out.

I adjust my bag strap, walk to the door, and step outside before she can recover.

The bell above the bistro door jingles.

It sounds like a cruel little joke.

chapter fifteen

I didn't realize I was smiling until my cheeks started to hurt a little—one of those small, quiet smiles that sneaks up on you when you're not paying attention.

Not the kind I forced for teachers or coworkers so they wouldn't ask if I was okay.

This one feels...real. Honest. Like something cracked open in my chest and let a little light through.

Jada had dragged me out to the park after my last class. "Just a walk," she'd said. "Stretch your legs, old man."

I almost bailed. Twice.

But when I came downstairs, there she was—sitting on the curb outside my building, mouthing lyrics to a song I didn't know, swinging her feet, looking up at me like she'd been waiting all day.

So here we are.

City lights shimmer on the river like someone shook a snow globe full of neon. The breeze smells like peppermint and early winter. Jada leans against the railing, sipping a cocoa stacked with enough whipped cream to cause structural concern, while I peel at the wrapper of a granola bar I'm not even hungry for.

"Better than the rink?" I ask, nudging his shoulder with mine.

He squints like he is thinking very seriously about it. "Depends. Can we skate on the river?"

"Only if we want to drown creatively."

He shoves my arm and I can't help it—I smile again. He makes everything feel lighter. Like someone loosens the knots in my chest without asking.

He takes another sip of his cocoa, then glances sideways at me.

"Hey... I talked to someone the other day. About you."

My stomach drops. The air doesn't feel as warm anymore.

"Who?" I ask.

They hesitate—barely, but enough.

"Viviana."

The smile dies instantly.

The wrapper tears clean in half between my fingers.

Jada's voice softens, almost too gentle. "She said she regrets what happened. That she didn't know how to fix it then, but she's trying to—"

"Why would you talk to her about me?" I snap, turning toward them.

"It's not like I went looking for her," they say quickly. "She came into the library right after you finished helping me with math. I didn't even know it was her at first, she just—she started talking, and it kind of happened. I didn't mean to tell her how you felt..."

I shake my head, backing up a step.

"No. Nope. We're not doing this."

"Payton—"

But I'm already walking away.

I don't know where I'm going, just that I have to move. I need space, fresh air, distance from the look on their face. From her voice saying Viviana's name like it didn't burn.

Jada follows me across the street, their boots slapping the pavement like they are trying to catch up to a runaway train.

"Wait—can we just talk about this?"

"You *are* talking," I mutter. "You're doing plenty of that."

"Don't do this. Don't shut down just because it's uncomfortable."

I spin around so fast they almost run into me. "Uncomfortable? This isn't uncomfortable, Jada—this is—" My voice cracks, humiliatingly. "It's like a betrayal."

Their expression crumple. "All we did was talk—"

"I don't care that you talked, talk to whoever you want, who am I to dictate that!?" The words keep coming out of me like someone had yanked a valve open. "The problem is you talked to her *about me*!"

"I just wanted to help—"

"I didn't ask for your help!"

Cars roll past behind her, headlights throwing short, sharp shadows over her face. She looks smaller in them. Or maybe I just feel bigger—louder—than I meant to be.

"You don't even know the half of it," I say. "You don't know what you're talking about."

"Then tell me!" she yells back. "Why can't you just let me in!"

"Because the last time I let someone in, they took away my future!"

She stops dead, like the words froze her in place.

I drag a hand through my hair, shaking. "I wanted—*God*—I wanted more than anything to go to MIT. We'd known each other for years. You'd think she would've known."

A laugh rips out of me, wild and empty. "But no, she didn't care about me that much. She never told me anything. And when she finally listened and found out I wanted to leave the state, she ruined my one chance at getting in. I worked on that project for five years, and she pulled the plug in five seconds. Literally. She stole my life away from me."

My voice is raw now. "And you think—" I choke on the words. "You think she's trying? She couldn't try when it mattered, so why the hell should I believe she's trying now?"

Jada just stares at me—wide-eyed, stunned—like I'd hit her.

"I didn't mean to hurt you," she whispers.

I look away, jaw tight enough to crack. "Then don't defend her."

"She's trying, Payton. She regrets what happened. Maybe she's not who she used to be."

"Just stop, Jada...please—" My voice betrays me, cracking again.

"Why can't you understand that Viviana may have changed?" he asks, stepping closer, softer now. "Because people can change. She could be better now. Maybe you'd see that if you just—"

And something inside me snaps.

"Because that means she could've always changed!" My hands clench at my sides. My breath shakes.. "And I just... I wasn't worth that."

The words hit the air like a brick through glass.

Jada doesn't say anything.

He doesn't move.

Doesn't breathe, almost.

My eyes burn, but I refuse to let anything fall. I stare down the street instead, anywhere but at him.

"I need to go."

"Payton, wait—"

"Goodbye, Jada...good luck at the tryouts."

And then I start walking.

Not fast.

Not running.

Just...leaving.

I don't look back.

chapter sixteen

I haven't left my room for three days.

Not for food, not for class, not even for the texts that keep lighting up my phone like tiny alarms I refuse to answer.

I saw them all—Jada's frantic ones, Vinny's blunt ones, even the polite "checking in" emails from my professor. I opened them, read them, then let them rot unanswered. It feels easier to disappear than explain why everything inside me feels scraped out.

The blinds stay shut, and so do I.

Same hoodie. Same sheets. Same stale forget-to-breathe air.

My computer sits on my desk like something from another life. I can't look at it.

I'm not angry anymore—anger takes energy.

I'm just tired.

Tired of thinking.

Tired of feeling like the villain in my own life.

Tired of pretending *my life* hadn't already *ended* last year.

The door creaks.

My mom steps in, slow and cautious, like my room is a wild animal. She sets a bowl of chili on the nightstand.

"It's cold out," she says softly. "You should eat."

I don't say anything.

She hovers. I could feel her working up to something.

"I know things are hard lately. But this isn't going to fix—"

"Don't."

Her eyebrows draw together. "Don't what?"

"Don't act like you care."

It hits her like a slap. "Payton—"

"No," I cut in, sitting up. "You don't get to show up with food and a soft voice and pretend like you haven't left me alone for the past year."

"Where is all this coming from?" she asks, moving into the room, picking up sweaters just to have something to do. She drops them into the laundry basket and sits at the edge of my bed. "You know I've been trying—"

"Trying?" I laugh—sharp and ugly. "You've been trying to pay bills. Trying to keep *yourself* upright. But you haven't been trying with *me*. You didn't even notice when I stopped caring. You didn't notice when I quit soccer. You didn't ask why I didn't go to MIT."

"I thought you changed your mind," she whispers.

"You should've asked!"

She reaches into her cardigan and pulls out a pamphlet. "I think it might be a good idea to try therapy again, Payt—"

"Are you serious right now?!"

"Yes," she says, firmer. "This behavior isn't healthy."

"Mom, I am basically crying for help from *you* right now, and you just—" I stop myself before I say something worse. "Sure. Just shove the problems you don't want to deal with onto other people. That's fine. Mother of the year."

Her voice snaps. "Do not speak to me that way, I'm the adult here—"

"Mom," I say, quiet but lethal. "*I've* been the adult here since Dad died."

She freezes.

"I'm the one who's been holding us together. I'm twenty. Twenty. And I'm tired. I am so *damn* tired."

She looks down at her hands like they have answers she'd forgotten how to read.

"You say you're trying. Trying to keep us in this apartment, keep us together... Then why am I the one paying half the rent? Why am I the one saving up so Austin can go to college? Why am *I* the one taking care of a seven-month-old girl? This isn't my job. I'm not a substitute parent!" My voice cracks, hoarse from crying more than yelling.

"I'm doing the best I can," she murmurs.

"Well, it's not enough."

Silence swallows the room.

I didn't wait for her to fill it.

I grab the first jacket off the chair and brush past her.

"Where are you going?" she asks, panicked.

"Out."

"It's almost midnight—"

"I don't care."

"It's freezing! It's supposed to storm! Please, let's talk abou—"

The door shuts harder than I meant it to.

The hallway air slaps me awake.

Cold. Sharp. Better than the soup. Better than the bed.

Better than being in that room one more second.

I shove my hands in my pockets and walk.

One destination. One away from here.

*. ❄ * ❄ *. ❄ .* ❄ * ❄ .*

I don't realize how far I've gone until the streetlamps grow sparse, the sidewalk turning more white, snow piling up as I walk. The last lamp flickers overhead, buzzing like it was shivering too.

The hoodie was a mistake.

The cold knives through it.

My fingers throb in my pockets, stiff and useless.

But I can't go back.

Back means facing her.

Back means all the things I can't hold anymore.

So I keep moving.

The burn in my chest isn't from the cold—it's from something trying to claw its way out. My breath comes out in broken puffs, like laughter without joy. Like sobs without sound.

I wipe my eyes on my sleeve, my cheeks sting as they are pelted with more snow.

"Get it together," I mutter.

I know the way. I always know the way.

Even though I hate this part of the night.

The quiet makes the memories loud.

I turn the corner.

There it is.

The intersection by the lake.

I freeze.

The snow had filled most of the cracks, but I still see them—

the jagged tear in the pavement,

the dented guardrail,

the ghost of a skid mark.

This is where he died.

Right here.

Because of me.

Didn't matter what Mom said.

Didn't matter what the police report said.

Didn't matter how many times people told me I was wrong.

I knew the truth.

I was the one yelling.

I was the one he turned toward.

I was the one who looked away from the road.

My breath hitches. Something slips out of my mouth—something slurred and broken, a sound more than a word.

I force myself forward.

Just a few more blocks to the cemetery.

Just a few.

Then—

Click.

My brace locks.

My left leg seizes mid-step, stiff as metal.

I pitch forward and catch myself against a nearby street sign.

"No. Nononono—!" I gasp, hitting the brace. "Not now. Come on—come on—"

My hands wouldn't listen.

My fingers barely move, cold and clumsy.

I drop onto one knee into a lunge, unable to move my other leg.

Snow crawls into my jeans, into my sleeves, up my spine.

I try to stand.

Failed.

I try to speak.

Nothing.

My vision tunnels.

My arms jerk like they are moving through wet cement.

My breath comes in tiny, useless sips.

I can't tell if I'm shaking from panic or cold.

I think of Dad.

How he used to pat my shoulder twice—always twice—after a good game.

How I used to cook with him.

How I couldn't remember his voice anymore, not clearly, not really—

Why couldn't I remember?

The tears come hot, then freeze on my cheek.

"Please," I choke. "*Please—*"

My body is collapsing in pieces.

Thoughts flicker out one by one.

This had been a mistake.

All of it.

I should've stayed home.

Should've swallowed everything down.

Should've never yelled in that car.

I never should've told Jada anything.

I should've kept pretending.

And now here I am—in the snow, locked in a body that won't move, my heart cracked wide open—and all I want is to talk to my dad.

Just one word.

One sign.

Something.

But the cemetery is still blocks away.

And this—this scarred sidewalk, this broken brace, where everything changed—

this is all I got.

I press my forehead to the snow.

"I'm sorry," I whisper, barely audible. "I'm so sorry. I didn't mean to—"

The world tilts.

I try to stand. One more time.

Tried to see the cemetery gate.

I didn't make it.

My body slumps sideways into the snow.

The cold doesn't hurt anymore.

I don't feel anything.

The shivering stops.

My chest barely moves.

My heartbeat flickers—slow, too slow—

My hands are blue at the edges.

The noise in my head fades.

Not because the fear left.

But because I did.

The last thing I see is the crack in the pavement.

The last thing I feel is the snow against my cheek.

I went still.

Alone.

Half-frozen beside the place that had haunted me for years.

And for one strange, fragile moment—

there is peace.

Then nothing.

chapter seventeen

The world comes back in pieces. Bright white light. A steady beep. Burn in my throat.

I blink, or try to—my eyelashes feel frozen shut.

The ceiling comes into view, then the quiet, sterile haze of the hospital room.

I am warm. Too warm. My skin itches beneath the blankets.

But the shaking is gone.

My chest still aches like it had been hit with bricks, but at least it's moving.

I turn my head, just slightly.

Jada is here.

He is curled in the corner chair with his knees hugged to his chest, earbuds tangled, one hand clutching a disposable coffee cup like it was his lifeline.

His eyes are puffy. Hair messy. No makeup. He looks like he hasn't slept in days.

I try to say her name, but it comes out rough—just a rasp of breath.

Jada sits up instantly. "Hey," she whispers. "Hey—no, no, don't. Your voice is still kinda- bad."

I try anyway. "You...?" She nods quickly.

"Yeah. I—I was coming to talk to you. Because I felt like shit. And then I saw you. You were just lying there, in the snow, and—" Her voice cracks. She blinks hard. "You scared the shit out of me."

My hand twitches against the sheet. I want to reach out, say something, anything.

"I know what you're gonna say," Jada says softly. "You're gonna apologize. For what you said. For storming off. For the stuff with Viviana."

I meet her eyes. She is right, she knows she is right. I see, just slightly, a flicker of amusement behind the exhaustion—she smiles. "I know," she whispers, eyes glassy.

I let my small, strained smirk stay for a second longer than I should've.

Then they reach forward and gently take my hand in theirs. It is the first thing in days that doesn't feel cold.

We sit like that for a minute before I croak, "The comp... how'd it go?"

Jada blinks in surprise, then their face lights up like a streetlamp in winter fog. "I made it," they say. "Round two. I—uh—passed."

Even with my chapped lips and cracked throat, I manage a tiny smile. It is crooked. Weak. But real. "Knew you would."

Their hand tightens around mine. "I'm sorry too," they say. "For getting involved—trying to convince you to do something that...you just can't do yet."

I don't pull away. They hold on tighter. "But Payton," they continue, their voice quiet, but firm, "people change. Whether they want to or not. Whether *you* want them to or not."

I stare at the wall. The IV. The blinking monitor. Anywhere but her face.

"I'm not asking you to forgive her. Or me." A pause. "Actually, that's the last thing I expect you to do."

I could feel my jaw start to clench.

"I just want you to acknowledge the change. That it exists. That it's possible."

The silence between us isn't heavy this time. Just quiet. Like the snow falling outside the window. Jada glances at the clock on the wall. Her shoulders droop a little. "I have to go. My flight leaves in a few hours."

I blink. It took effort. "Canada," I rasp.

He nods. "Winter break." He stands, slipping his hand from mine but letting his fingers drag across my palm a second longer.

"But I'll text you. Like, obnoxiously, even if you don't answer half the time. So get used to that."

I watch him gather his things, tug on his coat, and shove his coffee cup in the trash.

When he reaches the door, he pauses and looks back. "I'll see you in a few weeks."

The door clicks softly behind him.

I lay here for a long while after, staring at the ceiling.

The silence isn't screaming.

It just... is.

quarter 3

"I think you just gotta keep in mind that you're worthy of great things, independent of anyone who comes and goes in your life. Once you realize that, you're capable of feeling those feelings on your own terms."

– Thomas Sanders

chapter eighteen

Just sitting down makes my stomach twist. I try to look normal—whatever that means now—but if anyone looks close, they'd see it:

the way my jaw wouldn't unclench,

the way my shoulders lock up like my brace,

the death grip I have on the edge of the seat.

Thirty minutes of silence.

My mom doesn't say a single word.

And I don't want her to.

But the silence is brutal. It rattles around the car louder than any argument ever could.

What she thinks I don't know—what she doesn't want me to know—is that she's taking all of this as her fault. Not the snow. Not the brace malfunction. But everything leading up to it. Every moment she didn't catch until it was too late.

And the messed up part is...I *did* blame her.

Not for the accident.

But for everything else.

The overload. The exhaustion. The years of patching myself up alone.

And as much as I want to talk—deep down—I also want to get out of this car and never look at her again.

I feel humiliated knowing Jada saw me like that.

And worse?

I scared my mom. Again.

Almost the exact anniversary of the first accident.

Even the doctor had joked, "Let's not make this an annual tradition, okay?"

Yeah. *Hilarious.*

I try not to look out the window. Motion makes everything tilt.

The road makes me nauseous.

Even looking down makes it worse.

So I just...keep glancing at Mom, then closing my eyes, then looking again so I wouldn't fall asleep.

When we finally pull into the apartment lot, she clears her throat and says quietly,"I'll grab your crutch. Go up without me. I—" She stops. "I need to take a call."

I nod, but inside?

Inside I was boiling.

A call.

A CALL.

I just got out of the hospital and she's choosing a phone call?

Does she even care?

She opens the door for me, hands me my crutch, and I start hobbling inside. Every step feels like someone is wringing out my bones.

"Be careful getting to the elevator, okay?"

"Whatever..."

It slips out before I could stop it.

By the time I get upstairs, my hands are shaking from trying to juggle the crutch, keys, and pain. You'd think after a year or so of this, I'd be good at it. Nope.

I fumble with the lock three times before it turns.

The apartment is silent.

Too silent.

Austin isn't home.

Millie is with the neighbors...Mom can grab her later.

I go straight to my room.

The silence feels familiar in the worst way—like the night we came back after Dad died.

Like the quiet is a living thing, watching me, following me from room to room.

Every step I take echoes that same feeling in my chest—the dread, the heaviness, the cold, empty reminder that everything I used to be was gone.

I slam my bedroom door shut and flick on the fairy lights.

They glow a soft and warm blue.

It feels wrong.

Everything feels wrong.

My eyes drift to the NASA poster on the wall—the one I used to stare at for hours.

The one I used to talk about with Dad, planning everything we'd do once I got into MIT.

I look away.

Sit on my bed.

Set the crutch aside.

Lay down.

And all I can think about was how I failed.

Failed my dad.

Failed my mom.

Failed myself.

And the worst part is knowing there is no cure for that.

No doctor.

No therapy.

No reset.

Just me.

My eyes burn as tears well—slow at first, then faster.

But sadness only lasts a minute before something hotter takes its place.

Anger.

I push myself upright. My leg screams, but I don't stop.

I kneel on the edge of the bed, grab the poster and the ones around it, and rip it down.

The paper tears like a scream.

I shred it piece by piece.

Five years of work.

Five years of dreams.

Five years of planning.

Gone.

Just like that.

I stare at the scraps in my hands—torn stars, ripped equations, the little corner with the MIT logo I used to hit for luck.

The tears finally break loose for real.

I fall back onto my pillow, still clutching the shredded pieces like they were the last pieces of me.

Maybe they are.

My phone buzzes in my pocket. I wipe my face with the heel of my palm and pull it out.

Jada.

Of course.

She knows I was discharged today. She's checking in. And I appreciate it. I really do.

But I'm wrung out.

My chest feels hollow and bruised.

I stare at the screen, trying to think of a response.

A thumbs-up. A "yeah."

Anything.

But my thumbs won't move.

My head throbs.

My eyes are heavy.

Fine.

Whatever.

I put my phone down, grab my headphones, and shove them over my ears. I turn the volume up all the way. Was it a good idea? Absolutely not. But I don't care. I let the noise drown everything out. I turn on the playlist I made back when things were easier.

Back when I still believed in futures.

The music blasts.

Didn't help.

Didn't fix anything.

But at least it fills the silence.

chapter nineteen

Christmas comes and goes like a bad rerun.

New Year's, too—another countdown we all pretend not to hear.

The house feels smaller these days. Like the walls are inching in, waiting for someone to snap first. Mom keeps trying to pull me into conversations—soft ones, careful ones—but I couldn't do it. Every time she says, "Can we talk?" I feel something inside me slam shut.

So I avoid her. Easy enough when all you do is stay in your room.

Austin, though... he is the only one I couldn't hide from.

It finally hit the breaking point on a Wednesday. Or maybe it was Thursday. All the days have started blending like dirty watercolor.

I'm sitting at the kitchen table, pretending to scroll my phone, when Austin walks in. He looks like he hasn't slept, jaw tight enough to crack.

"Are you seriously still ignoring Mom?" he asks.

I don't look up. "Not everything has to be a conversation."

He laughs—short, sharp. "Yeah? Well, maybe it should be."

I keep scrolling, scrolling, scrolling—

Then, suddenly, my phone is yanked out of my hands.

"Hey—what the hell!?"

Austin slams it onto the counter. "I'm done, Payton. I'm done watching you rot in this house."

My stomach drops. "What are you talking about?"

"You," he snaps. "Giving up. On everything."

I'm about to say something but he doesn't stop.

"You used to actually try. You used to care about school, about your projects, about—about life." His voice shakes with anger he'd clearly been holding in for weeks. "Now you won't even go outside unless it's to wander into a snowstorm and nearly freeze to death!"

"That was one time—"

"Oh my god, listen to yourself!" He throws his hands up. "You almost died, Payton! And you act like it was a walk to the mailbox!"

I look away. My heart is pounding, but my face stays empty.

"You used to fight for things," he says, quieter now but more dangerous. "What happened to you?"

I feel the hit in my chest but don't show it.

Austin doesn't stop.

"Just because Dad's life is over," he says, voice cracking, "doesn't mean yours has to be too."

The air freezes. Even the fridge hums quieter.

I swallow, throat tight. "You don't know what you're talking about."

"Bullshit. You think you're the only one who lost him? You think you're the only one who gets to fall apart?" He shakes his head. "We all did, Payton. But you're the only one who refuses to get back up."

He storms down the hallway before I could respond, leaving me alone with the kind of silence you can drown in.

*. ❄ * ❄ *. ❄ .* ❄ * ❄ .*

Tonight, Mom tries again.

I'm walking past her in the living room when she says softly, "Payton...stop. Please."

I freeze, jaw clenching. "Mom, I'm tired. I don't want to do this."

"Well," she says, standing up, "I think we have to."

Something in her voice makes me turn. She isn't soft this time. She isn't careful. She looks...exhausted. Scared.

"What do you want me to say?" I mutter.

"I want you to stop pretending you're fine when you're not."

I let out a humorless laugh. "You're one to talk."

Her face falls, but she doesn't look away. "You're right." She takes a shaky breath. "I have been pretending...I felt like I had to..."

"Why?" I hiss. "I'm not a child, you don't have to treat me like one!"

"Because admitting it wasn't it—" her voice breaks. "It felt like I would be giving up on him completely."

My chest tightens. For once, I don't fire back.

"I didn't know how to help you," she says. "So I tried to act like we were... normal. Like nothing had changed. But it did. Everything did."

I stare at her, something tugging behind my ribs. "You should've said that earlier."

"I know." Her eyes are glassy but steady. "I just... I didn't want to watch you hurt."

"Well," I whisper, "I was hurting anyway."

We stand here, stuck between the things we'd never said and the things we finally were.

It isn't a full fix. Not even close.

But it is the first honest step either of us had taken in a long, long time.

chapter twenty

I texted Esme because I needed to get out of the house. I needed space—distance—from the mess of the last few weeks. Things with my family were getting better, I could feel that much, but I needed them to get better slowly. And slowing things down... that was something I could actually control.

I walk into town with my earbuds in, music cranked just enough to tune out everything. A block away from the bistro, I stop and scan the sidewalk, trying to spot Esme. That's when I feel a tap on my shoulder—one single pink nail in my peripheral vision.

I whip around.

"Hi! Did I scare ya?" she asks, way too enthusiastically.

"No!" I blurt—too quick. Too defensive.

She laughs. "You know, I'm really glad you texted me."

"Really?"

"Yeah, I was starting to think you deleted my contact." She laughs again. "Oh! Also, another one of my friends asked to hang out today and he's at the bistro right now... are you cool if he joins us?"

I hesitate—hard.

What if it's someone who hates me?

What if it's someone who used to bully me?

Worst of all—what if it's someone completely new? New people are terrifying.

But I don't want to be the buzzkill.

"Sure," I stutter.

Esme lights up. Her smile could've powered the entire block. She grabs my hand and pulls me toward the bistro.

"Don't be worried about anything. He's really nice. I think you guys are gonna hit it off pretty well!"

She sounds like an elementary school teacher comforting the new kid on their first day. I try to settle the nerves buzzing in my chest, but I don't really know what to expect.

The bell above the bistro door jingles as we walk in. Vincent waves from behind the counter, talking to some guy with split-dye hair—black and purple. Something about it tugs at a memory.

When the guy turns around, he sees Esme first.

"There's my girl!" he calls, in a voice way deeper than I expected from someone who looks that soft.

"Hi E—"

"Elio...?" I say before I can stop myself. I regret it immediately.

Elio's head snaps toward me. His eyes widen.

"Holy—Payton?! Damn man, how you been?" He walks over and sticks out his hand.

"I—fine—" I stutter, taking it to give him a handshake as he pulls me into a hug instead, throwing me absolutely off-balance.

"You two know each other?" Esme asks.

"We played soccer at Sierra! You should've seen 'em!" Elio throws an arm around me, tugging me closer. "Best player I'd ever seen."

I quickly step away. "It wasn't all that—"

"Are you kidding? We won at state because of you!"

I shrug, trying not to look like I was choking on nostalgia. I missed it. God, I missed it. Playing again felt impossible—my leg, the way I walked now, the way everything was tied to Dad. It feels wrong to even imagine stepping on a field again.

"Really, it was nothing..."

"Whatever you say," Elio laughs, moving back over to Esme. "So what's the plan for today, love?"

"I was just thinking we could all hang here," she says. "I just know I could use a quiet day with people before I have to go back to work..." She chuckles.

"Working with high schoolers, much less early college students, is insane. I don't know how you do it." Elio sighs.

"Wait, you teach at an Early College?" I ask. "Which one?"

"I actually teach at Sierra!" she smiles. "Your brother is in my chemistry class."

I blinked and followed her toward the counter. "How'd you know about—?"

"You both look very similar and you have the same last name. It wasn't super hard to put together," she said with a giggle. Guess it's good to put the name Ms. Kumar to a face.

We went up to the counter together and ordered: her Raspberry Iced Matcha with Cold Foam, my Matcha.

When we sit back down with Elio, I watch the two of them talk—effortless, natural. I envy that. I used to have that with Jada. I didn't have it with anyone else. Not even Mom.

Vincent brought our drinks over and walked off.

"Payton! Matcha twins!" Esme exclaims, clinking her cup lightly against mine before taking a sip.

"Ugh, now there's two of you," Elio groans. "Matcha is gross and I stand by that."

"And what did you get?" I ask, smugly.

"Iced Mocha Dark Roast," he replies, taking a long sip.

I physically recoiled. Esme immediately started arguing with him about how that was the worst kind of coffee ever invented—besides black coffee—and Elio pushed back about matcha being swamp water. They went back and forth, dramatic and ridiculous, and I just watched.

It felt...nice. Just being there.

Eventually, Elio throws his hands up. "Fine, fine. We can agree to disagree."

Esme sticks her tongue out at him—gracefully, somehow—and he laughs.

"So, how'd you two meet?" I ask. "You seem like you've known each other for a while."

"We met when Essie got lost in the halls of SEC going to a football game," Elio says.

"It was my first and only year in cheer since I was graduating early, and I'd never been to a sports event at another school before—"

"This was our sophomore year, by the way," Elio cut in.

"AND," she emphasizes, "I was trying to get to the soccer game, which is where I met Elio because someone was running late and bumped into me in the hall."

She shoots him a look.

"Wait—I remember that. Coach was pissed at you," I snort.

"Oh really?"

"Yep. Our first varsity game and he's late. He was benched for two weeks."

Elio flushes. "Well—let's not dwell on the past! And I'll have you know JV started later than Varsity. Not my fault."

There was a comfortable silence for a moment.

"So… Elio," I say. "What have you been doing since EC?"

"Oh! I'm a tattoo artist!" he says proudly. "Well, technically I'm still an apprentice, but I'm getting my license in a few weeks, so consider me a real artist."

"That's really cool—do you have a place? Maybe I could stop by sometime?"

"Hell yeah! Come by Madeline's. It's on West 53rd."

I type the address into my phone and slide it toward him. "Realized I never actually had your number."

He grins, picking it up, entering his contact info.

Esme suddenly asks, "So, what made you text me after all this time? If you're okay with me asking."

I hesitate. "I just… I wanted to feel normal again."

She tilts her head. "What do you mean?"

"I just—needed something that didn't involve everything else."

"I get that…" She pauses. "How's Jada?"

"I—don't know… I haven't really—reached out in a while…"

"Payton!"

"I know, I know! It's just been hard… these past few weeks haven't exactly been sunshine and rainbows."

"Look, I don't know exactly how you feel—but I get the concept," she said. "You can't ghost her forever."

"I know…"

"Do you?" Elio chimes in.

I frown. "What do you mean by that?"

"I mean—I was gonna text myself from here so I have your number, and I saw that there are unread texts from Jada from December 26th to now."

"You read them?!" I snatch my phone.

"No! That's not my business—but it's January 10th. If you haven't even read some of them... did you have any intention of getting back to her at all?"

"You don't know me."

"No, but I remember you," he shoots back. "Once everything happened with Viviana, you shut everybody out. Not even coach could reach you. I think Jackson said he messaged you every day for two months and you didn't say a word. You just kinda ghosted everybody. Then you didn't come to school for—like—ever. People thought you died. The amount of slacked jaws I saw when you walked the grad stage? Insane."

"That was different—that wasn't just about Viviana..."

"Payton, I know what it was about," he says softly. "The whole soccer team knew. The school didn't—but we did. You have this habit of shutting people out when things get bad."

"And," Esme emphasizes, again, trying to ease the slight tension, "while it's okay to take time for yourself," Esme adds, "it's not okay to isolate yourself completely. It's not just hard for your friends—it's hard on you."

"But that— I didn't know what to do then. I...I lost everything. My future, part of my hearing, partial function in my leg, my dad! Just—everything fell to pieces..."

Esme froze. She hadn't known.

"I know this isn't the same," I whisper. "But it feels the same. Which is why this is so—"

"It's hard," Elio says quietly.

I nod.

Esme takes my hand gently. "No one said it would be easy...but you'll get through it. You've survived 100% of your bad days. You've got this one way or another."

She squeezes my hand and stands. "I'm gonna get another coffee. You want one?"

I smile at her.

And that was the moment I knew keeping her number had been a good idea.

chapter twenty-one

I always know when I'm dreaming.
Everything feels like it's underwater—slow,
echoing, like my own memories are trying to
talk to me. And tonight, the dream drags me
right into junior year. Right into the beginning
of the end.

*The science lab looks exactly the same: burnt
solder, chemical cleaner, and the specific brand of panic
that belongs solely to teenagers messing with electricity.
I'm hunched over my fuel-conversion system, the
early-stage model of the rocket booster, a mess of
equations and wiring diagrams spread around me like
some kind of altar.*

I hear the door creak before I see her.

*"Payt?" Viviana's voice floats in, soft and a little
teasing. "It's the first week of school. Who voluntarily
stays in the lab this late? You got a project already?"*

I don't look up right away—I'm soldering a connection. "Hey." I smiled at her. "And it's not a school project. It's the college thing, remember?"

"College thing?" she repeats, and there's this dip in her tone. Confusion. Something tight.

"MIT. The sustainable propulsion program." I give a tiny laugh. "I swear I've talked your ear off about it."

She tries to smile, but it twitches at the corner. She steps closer, tugging one of her sleeves. "Right. Yeah. Sorry. Long day."

I straighten up, stretch my back, turn to her. That's when I see it—the quick flicker in her eyes when I say MIT. Worry. Fear. Something she thinks she's hiding well.

"Hey," I say gently. "It's not like if I get in, I disappear."

She shrugs like she's fine but her shoulders stay raised. "It's far...what if—"

"A couple hours," I remind her, trying to ease her mind. "I can visit. You can visit. We'll figure it out."

She nods, but the room cools a little. Even dream-me feels that shift. I didn't understand it then. I sure as hell understand it now.

The dream fast-forwards—like someone dragging a timeline bar.

Middle of first semester. The morning of the interview.

I'm back in the lab, nerves vibrating under my skin like high voltage. I'm double-checking every circuit, every wire, testing the small-scale booster's fuel conversion chamber. Everything runs clean. It hums exactly how it's supposed to. Perfect.

Viviana pokes her head in the doorway. "You're doing great," she says, even though I haven't said anything. "You always do great."

I grin. "You sound more nervous than me."

She laughs—too sharp, too breathy. I don't catch it in real time. But in the dream, I watch her eyes flick toward the project. Then away. Then back.

And then the dream cuts again.

I'm standing in the hall with three judges—one professor from MIT, one engineer from Jet Propulsion, and one admissions rep who's so serious she might actually be carved from stone.

"After you," I say, holding the door open, trying not to sprint ahead.

My project sits centered on the workbench like a promise. The rocket model, small but functional, gleams under the fluorescent lights. Everything looks exactly how I left it.

I launch into my explanation. "This is a sustainable conversion prototype—the idea is to recycle the waste heat generated during launch into supplemental propulsion. If applied to full-scale—"

The professor nods. The engineer raises his brows, impressed. My heart lifts. This could be it. This could literally change everything.

"And if I may," I say, flipping the safety cover off the activation switch. "I can show you the live reaction cycle right here."

I hit the switch.

The system sparks. Then coughs. Then dies.

A thin plume of smoke curls up like a taunt.

My brain drops straight through the floor. "No, no, this worked last night—hang on—"

I open the side panel. My fingers freeze.

A wire—one of the main conductive lines—is cleanly snipped.

Not frayed.

Not pulled loose.

Cut.

"Someone tampered with this," I say quickly, desperately, turning to them. "I swear, this was functioning. Please—let me reattach it and—"

"We appreciate your time," the stone-faced admissions rep says, already turning away.

"Please," I repeat. But it doesn't matter. They've seen enough.

They leave. The door swings shut with a soft click that feels like a guillotine.

My chest caves inward. I want to sink to the floor, curl up, disappear, scream. Something. Anything.

But then I hear it—soft crying from the hallway.

I wipe my face, push everything down, and step outside.

Viviana stands against the lockers, clutching her hands to her chest like she's breaking apart.

"Viv?" I say, rushing over. "Hey—whoa, what's going on? Are you hurt—?"

She shakes her head, sobbing harder.

That's when I see it.

The wire cutters. In her hand.

Everything inside me goes very, very still.

"Viv," I whisper. "What...what is that?"

"I— it wasn't..." She stumbles over her words. "I didn't mean—it was an accident—I was just—I was scared—I thought—if you went so far away—I panicked, Payton, I'm sorry—I'm so, so sorry—"

My heart doesn't just break.

It drops.

Like a trapdoor with no bottom.

"You cut it?" My voice cracks.

She sobs harder. "I didn't think—I didn't mean for it to ruin everything—I swear—"

"You took—" I swallow hard.

"I'm sorry," she whispers again, like it fixes anything.

I go to say something—wanting to yell, to ask why, to tell her how much that project meant to me. But nothing comes out. Nothing feels big enough to hold everything crushing my chest.

So I just shake my head.

And I walk away.

The only thing I manage, when she calls after me, voice shattering:

"I don't want to see you right now."

And I mean it.

But dreams don't let you leave cleanly.

Spring semester hits hard and cold.

Viviana tries for student council again—senior-year leadership, big deal, shiny college applications, all of it. Even after everything, she corners me after class.

"Payton," she says, not quite meeting my eyes. "Can you... get the soccer team to show up to Spring Fling? You're the captain, if you ask them, they'll definitely be there...and it'll guarantee my spot."

I want to say no.

I should say no.

But I'm not her. I'm not vindictive.

"Yeah," I tell her quietly. "I'll help. I'm not trying to mess with your future."

She nods, relieved. "Thank you."

Except the soccer team never shows.

I got a text—date moved. But that was a lie.

And that Monday morning, I was back in the lab, fixing one of the vents, when she stormed in.

"YOU PROMISED!" Her voice cracks the air. "You said they'd come! Do you have any idea what this did to my chances?!"

"Viv— what are you talking about, they changed the date—"

"Don't lie to me!"

"I'm not lying!" I say, louder than I mean to. "This isn't my fault, look—"

And then she slaps me.

We both freeze.

Her eyes widen with immediate horror. "Payt—I didn't—I didn't mean—I'm sorry—I'm so sorry—"

I take a step back. My cheek throbs, but it's my heart that feels bruised.

"Believe whatever you want," I say quietly. "I'm done with this."

I walk—

Viviana breaking apart on the other side.

The dream holds me there for a moment.

In the hallway. In the silence.

Then everything blurs, dissolves, collapsing back into darkness.

I stopped believing in people after that.

chapter twenty-two

I didn't think texting Jada would feel like trying to bench-press a car. But here I am, staring at my phone like it might bite me.

After hanging out with Esme and hearing her talk about actually communicating, actually showing up instead of hiding, something cracked open in my chest. Something uncomfortable and overdue. And all the messages from Jada I'd left on read... they hit different after talking with Esme.

So I finally text her. Just a quick:

Hey. Could we meet at the rink?

I expect nothing. Maybe a one-word reply. Or a three-day wait, which, honestly, I deserve.

But she responds in under a minute with:

Yeah. What time?

My stomach drops. I give her a time. Then I stare at my reflection in the bathroom mirror for a good five minutes like a clown.

By the time I get to the rink, my nerves are doing laps.

The place is mostly empty—the kind of quiet echo that makes every sound feel louder. I sit on the bleachers and bounce my leg because apparently that's my entire personality now.

I keep going over everything I want to say in my head, and it all sounds wrong, or weird, or too much. I shouldn't be this nervous. It's Jada. But my body doesn't care. It's like someone stuck a hive of bees in my chest.

The doors squeak open.

Jada walks in.

They look...nervous too. Cautious, but warm. That mix they get when they're not sure whether they should brace for impact or relax. They give a tiny wave, almost shy.

"Hey," they say.

"Hey," I say, but mine comes out more like a croak.

They sit beside me, leaving just enough space that I could fill it if I were brave. They tuck a curl behind their ear, eyes flicking up at me, then away.

"So," he says softly.

"So," I echo, because apparently I forgot how to human.

I swallow, drag in a breath. "I... uh. I've been thinking. A lot. And I know I haven't really given you anything. Like...at all. And you've texted me so much and I just—I didn't know how to—I wasn't trying to ignore you, I just—"

I stop because he's already smiling.

Not smug.

Not triumphant.

Just...warm. Understanding. Like he already knows what I'm trying to say and he's relieved to finally hear me try.

He reaches out, gently, and takes my hand like he's testing whether I'll pull away.

I don't.

He stands up and tugs me with him—not hard, just enough to make me follow. Then he pulls me straight into his arms.

I freeze for half a second, because my brain short-circuits, but then I melt into it. She's soft and warm and smells like her mango-something shampoo.

Her chin rests on my shoulder. Her fingers grip the back of my hoodie like she's been holding this in for weeks.

"I missed you," she whispers.

The words hit me like a punch and a rescue at the same time.

Then she laughs a small, breathy, relieved laugh against my chest and somehow that's what finally lets my heart unclench.

chapter twenty-three

But Jada does. More and more lately. And as much as it lights something warm in my ribs every time they text me first, or swing by after class, or ask if I want to hang out again—I'm not used to this. Not used to someone being around this much.

My life for the past two years has pretty much been:

school → home → silence.

Rinse. Repeat.

So having someone next to me on my couch with their knee almost touching mine, their hoodie sleeve brushing me whenever they shift? It's...yeah. It's a lot. But not in a bad way. Just in a holy crap my heart is doing parkour way.

They're looking around my room when it happens.

"Hey," Jada says softly. "What happened here?"

I follow their gaze to the two blank rectangles on my wall. The places where the NASA poster used to be. Where the soccer pictures were.

My stomach tenses. "I, uh... took them down."

Jada moves closer to the wall, fingertips hovering like they can still feel the edges of everything I ripped away. "Why?"

I shrug, sinking deeper into myself. "Didn't feel right anymore."

They glance at me and I can tell they already know that's only the surface. They sit on the edge of my bed, leaning in until their shoulder touches mine. Their presence is steady, soft.

"It's about your dad, isn't it?" they ask gently.

I freeze. A crack opens in my chest, just wide enough for the ache to slip out.

"Maybe," I whisper.

Jada doesn't push. They just wait—patient in a way that makes me want to talk and hide all at once.

I swallow hard. "He helped me pick those pictures. The poster too. We made playlists together. Like... all the time. For everything. Road trips, study days, first day of school." My throat gets tight. "Taking them down felt easier than seeing them."

Jada's face softens. "Payton...you don't have to erase him to move on."

I look away, blinking fast. "It felt like the only option."

They stand up suddenly. "Get Austin."

"What? Why?"

"Because," they say, crossing their arms in that stubborn way they do when they've already decided something, "you shouldn't do this alone."

And before I can argue, they're halfway to the living room calling, "Austin! Get in here!"

Austin drags himself out of his room, annoyed. "Why are you yelling—" Then he sees my face and sighs. "Oh."

Jada points to the storage bin under my bed. "*Payton*" they emphasize, "is taking a look at some of his old stuff."

I groan. "Do we have to?"

"Yes," Jada and Austin say at the same time.

So we dump everything out—old CDs, crumpled ticket stubs, little notes my dad used to tuck into my backpack, a broken keychain rocket. And while Jada sits cross-legged on the floor sorting through things, he goes, "Let's build him a new playlist."

For a second, my chest glows.

But then every song feels wrong. Too happy. Too slow. Too empty. Too full. I get irritated, then frustrated, then the frustration curdles into panic.

"I can't—" My breath stutters. "I can't make it fit. Nothing fits. Nothing sounds like him. I just want it back. I want—"

I shut my eyes. The ache is rising fast, like I'm drowning in it.

Jada moves quickly, kneeling in front of me and wrapping his arms around my shoulders before I can pull away. His forehead rests against my cheek.

"It's okay," he whispers. "It's okay. You don't have to force anything. I miss stuff too."

I swallow, shaky. "Like what?"

He breathes out, slow and heavy. "My birth-mom used to dance with me in the kitchen. Every Friday. No music, just whatever humming was stuck in her head." His voice softens. "I miss that. So much."

I don't know how long we stay like that pressed together on the floor, our grief carefully overlapping instead of colliding.

Then Austin reaches into a box and goes, "Uh...what's this?"

He holds up a VHS tape. MY BOYS written in our dad's handwriting.

My heart stops.

"Put it in," I whisper.

Austin loads it into the old player, the TV humming to life. And then

There he is.

My dad. Younger than I remember him. Holding Austin as a newborn. Laughing with Mom while I streak through the frame wearing a superhero cape. More clips show up, different years. Birthday candles. Soccer games. Christmas, two years ago now—the last one we spent together...

I sit forward, breath shaking. I pick up the case and a folded stack of notes slips out.

My dad's handwriting.

Little messages. Memories. Jokes. Things he wanted us to remember. Things he didn't want to forget.

It hits me all at once, a mix of relief and pain and something else I haven't felt in years. Something almost like warmth.

I don't cry, but something in me loosens.

For the first time, talking about him doesn't feel like picking at a wound. It feels...possible.

Later, when I walk Jada to the lobby, the air between us feels different, warmer, heavier in a good way. My chest flutters every time their sleeve brushes mine.

She shifts on her feet. "Hey…actually, do you wanna come to a group hang? Rosa, Valerie, a few others."

My knee jerks into an instinctive no.

But instead, I just sigh. "Yeah. Okay."

Jada laughs under her breath.

*. ❄ * ❅ *. ❆ .* ❅ * ❄ .*

Jada and Rosa's dorm feels like walking into a party I wasn't technically invited to but somehow ended up at anyway. Warm lights, bright colors, mismatched throw pillows, the smell of popcorn, and me, standing weirdly close to the wall like I'm waiting for a secret service extraction team.

Jada walks in like this really is her home, smiling, greeting people, dropping her bag by her bed. I hover near the door like it's my emotional support exit.

Rosa spots me first.

"PAYTONNNN!" she practically screams, waving her arms like she's guiding a plane in.

I flinch. "Hey."

She barrels over, grinning, eyes flicking to my ear as her hands start flying in gestures that look a little too intentional to just be excitement "You made it! Oh my god, this is so good. Jada said you might flake—"

"ROSA." Jada cuts in, giving her a death glare and reaching over to steady her moving hands.

Rosa shrugs and flips her hand up. "What?"

She's chaos in human form—loud, bright, the type who probably yells through text messages. She's so much like Jada in energy that it's almost funny. It's like meeting the extended version of them.

Valerie is next. Quiet smile, soft sweater, warm eyes. She gives a tiny wave.

"Hi. I've heard a lot about you," she says.

"Oh...sorry?" I say. She laughs.

And then there's Logan.

I don't know why, but the second she looks at me, calm, steady, this quiet little half-smile, my nerves loosen a little. Enough to breathe.

"So you're Payton," she says gently, as if confirming I am in fact a rare meteor or something.

"Last time I checked," I mutter.

She laughs. It's soft. Natural. Easy.

God, being around people who don't demand anything feels like stepping into the rain.

We all sit in a loose circle in the middle of the room. Well *they* sit in a circle. I sit partially behind a potted plant. Still visible. Technically.

Conversation bounces around:

Rosa complaining about her math teacher, Valerie hyping up some indie emo movie, Jada arguing with Logan about whether there was water on Mars (there is).

I watch them, quiet, absorbing the way they all talk over each other without ever clashing. Jada jumps topic-to-topic like a pinball, and Valerie is right there following them, answering or rolling their eyes or nudging their shoulder.

It's weirdly comforting. Like watching two people share one WIFI connection.

Jada glances back at me now and then, little checks, little smiles, and every time it feels like warmth unfurling across my ribs.

At some point, Rosa tosses a popcorn kernel at my head. She raises her eyebrows at me and grins, and without speaking this time, starts moving her hands. Sign Language, I think?

I guess I look like a lost puppy for a bit too long, so she shrugs and starts in English again. "You're too quiet," she says. "Say something, start a fight."

The room turns to me, Jada elbowing Rosa who throws her hands up in what looks like sideways jazz hands in response.

What does she mean? What should I say?

My brain immediately shorts out and the first thing that escapes is:

"Uhm—I think people who drink iced black coffee might be unwell."

Logan's eyes widen. "You hurt me."

"You drink iced matcha dark roast," Jada says. "You don't count."

"It's in the same category!" Logan protests.

"It's literally not," Valerie sighs.

Everyone dissolves into laughter, me included. Small, awkward, but nice.

It feels...okay.

More than okay.

There's a little pocket of space here where the air doesn't hurt to breathe.

When things wind down, I realize I've been there almost two hours. A personal record for Socializing While Emotionally Malfunctioning.

Jada brushes my arm. "Ready?"

"Yeah."

We all shuffle toward the exit. I'm in front, reaching for the door, when I hear whispering behind me, suspicious whispering, the kind accompanied by shoves and evil giggling.

I turn just in time to see Rosa literally pushing Jada forward like a kindergartener trying to send their friend to ask the teacher a question.

Jada stumbles, cheeks flushed. "Okay, STOP—go away—oh my god—"

Rosa scampers off, giggling. Jada shakes their head and approaches me.

Suddenly we're standing closer than normal. Close enough to feel their breath ghost over my shoulder. Close enough that something in my chest trips over itself.

They clear their throat, rummaging awkwardly in their bag. "So...uh..."

Their hands fidget, which is weird because Jada never fidgets unless she's really nervous.

It makes my stomach twist.

"There's this dance. In spring." They pull out a small envelope decorated with purple stars. "I, uh...wanted to give you this."

They press it into my hand, fingers brushing my knuckles, warm and hesitant.

"Just...think about it," they say softly, eyes flicking up to mine. "No pressure."

Before I can respond, before I can even inhale properly, they step forward and wrap their arms around me.

It's gentle at first, like they're checking if I'll tense. And I do. My whole body goes stiff like someone hit the freeze button.

But then Jada relaxes into the hug, their cheek against my shoulder, arms looping tighter and something in me unknots. Slowly. Carefully.

I breathe them in.

Warm. Soft. Familiar.

They pull back, smiling in this shy, hopeful way that makes something bloom in my chest.

"Night, Payton."

They turn and go back to the group before I can say anything. Rosa yells something. Logan elbows Jada. Valerie waves.

And I'm left in the doorway, holding the envelope, my heart performing Olympic gymnastics.

I don't move. I barely blink.

Then—

BZZZT.

My phone lights up.

A text from Austin.

Mom wants to talk. Now.

And just like that the warmth shatters, replaced by a heavy, familiar sinking.

Reality returns like cold rain.

I swallow, pocket the envelope, and head home.

chapter twenty-four

When I walk into the apartment, Austin's already sitting at the kitchen counter like he's guarding the entrance. Arms crossed. Jaw set. Mom's in the living room, pacing that tight, anxious pacing she does when she's trying not to cry or yell or both.

The second she sees me, she stops.

"Payton," she says, quiet but firm. "Sit down. Please."

I drop my bag. My pulse is a jackhammer. I sit.

Austin stays standing, which feels unfair like he's the prosecution and I'm the defendant.

Mom folds her hands together. "We need to talk. Really talk."

I let out a breath, sharp. "Yeah. I figured."

She opens her mouth, closes it again, then finally asks. "Where have you been? Why didn't you answer me?"

I shrug. "I was out."

"'Out' could mean anything," she snaps, emotion cracking her voice. "After everything—Payton, I can't go hours without knowing where you are. I can't."

Austin jumps in, frustrated. "It's like you don't care! Like you think you're invincible."

"That's not true, and you know I was with Jada, why do you even care?" I mutter.

"Are you serious?" Austin throws his hands up. "I care because you nearly froze to death in the snow last time you 'went out.' And when we try to help, you shut us out like we're the enemy."

My jaw tightens. "Maybe I don't need everyone hovering over me all the time."

"Hovering?" Austin barks. "Dude, we're trying to keep you alive."

Mom presses her palms to her eyes, shaking. "Stop. Both of you."

But the heat is already rising in my chest boiling, crowding my ribs.

Austin stares at me, chest heaving. "Why are you doing this? Why do you keep acting like you're the only one hurting?"

That does it.

"Because I am!" I snap. "Because *neither* of you get it!" I stand so fast the chair screeches.

Mom looks up, confused. "Get what?"

The words tear out before I can stop them.

"That it's my fault."

Silence hits the room like a dropped brick.

Austin blinks. "What?"

I swallow, but the lump in my throat won't move. "That night. The accident. *I* was driving—not Dad. I was the one behind the wheel. I should've— I should've done something. I should've seen the truck. I should've—"

My voice cracks, ugly and loud. "If I wasn't so tired, or mad, or—I don't know. Dad would still be here. And you—" I gesture helplessly between them. *"You wouldn't be falling apart."*

Mom's face softens in a way that makes everything worse. She stands slowly, like she's afraid I'll run.

"Payton," she whispers, "No."

"I killed him."

The words hang in the air, jagged.

Mom covers her mouth, tears streaming. Austin looks stunned, grief pouring over his features like someone pulled a rug out from under him.

Then Mom crosses the room and grabs my face in her hands, firm, shaking.

"Listen to me." Her voice trembles but does not break. "You did *not* kill your father."

"I was driving."

"You we're hit by a truck, into a lake!" she says. "That driver ran a red light—it could've happened to anyone."

"But it didn't happen to *anyone*," I choke. "It happened to *us*."

Mom pulls me into her arms. I stand stiff at first, hands hanging uselessly at my sides—until she speaks into my shoulder.

"I thought I'd lost you, too," she says, breath shaking. "When they called me that night and—and saw you in that hospital bed...I thought I'd lose the both of you."

I shut my eyes, pain spiking through my chest.

"You've always been the strong one," she continues. "Always the one holding things together. And I...I didn't realize I was letting you carry all of that alone."

My throat caves. I make a sound—raw, broken and suddenly I'm grabbing her back, fists bunching in her shirt like I'm seven again and hiding from thunderstorms.

Austin steps forward, voice soft for the first time. "You scared us, dude. You scare us when you disappear into your head."

Mom strokes the back of my head like she used to after nightmares. "I don't want to hover. I just want you safe. I want you here."

I'm crying now—actually crying hot, embarrassing tears that drip down her shoulder. I can't stop. I don't try to.

"I'm trying," I manage. "I just...don't know how—"

"That's okay," Mom whispers. "We'll figure it out together."

There's a long silence.

Finally, Mom pulls back just enough to look at me. "Will you let us help you now? Really let us?"

I sniff. "What do you mean?"

"I talked to someone," she says gently. "A therapist. And...the Resilience Institute has programs for trauma recovery—teenagers especially. They have an opening. I think it could help...it's not a punishment. Just...a reset. A place to learn how to breathe again."

I wipe my face with my sleeve, exhausted and hollowed-out. But something eases like a knot pulled loose.

"Yeah," I whisper. "I'll try. I'll go."

Mom's shoulders collapse in relief. She hugs me again, and this time I lean into it without fighting it.

Austin bumps my shoulder once she lets go. "Good," he says softly. "About time."

I let out a shaky, almost-laugh. "Shut up."

"Love you too," he smirks.

And for the first time in months, maybe longer, I feel like I'm not standing alone in a burning house.

Just...breathing. With them.

Together.

chapter twenty-five

The rink is loud in that soft way—blades whispering across ice, the hum of the lights, scattered applause echoing like distant bells. But none of it touches me. Not really.

Because she's out there again.

Jada's second performance. Her comeback. Her round two.

She glides onto the ice with that tiny, nervous smile she only lets slip when she thinks no one's looking. But she knows I'm looking. She glances toward the stands, a flicker of gold-brown eyes meeting mine and my chest does this stupid leap like I'm sixteen and someone said my name on the morning announcements.

The music starts.

And she moves.

Sharp. Fluid. Unapologetic. Like the ice itself is lucky to hold her weight. She cuts through the cold with a confidence so bright I almost forget how scared I'd been the first time she fell. The blood on her knees. How much silence afterward.

"She's okay," I whisper to myself, breath fogging the air. "She's okay."

Then it happens—the moment everyone's been waiting for.

Jada speeds up, pulling power from somewhere deep, and launches into a double axel.

Time slows.

She spins—clean, centered, light as breath.

She lands it, perfect.

And I'm on my feet before I can think, clapping so hard my palms sting like they're burning. I shout their name. I don't care who hears. They did it.

When the music ends, the applause fills the rink. Mine is the loudest. They bow, cheeks flushed, chest rising fast.

And they look at me again this time with fire.

When they reach me afterward, they don't even hesitate. Jada barrels into my arms, hugging me tight enough that my ribs complain but I don't dare move. I forget to breathe. It feels like being anchored and lifted all at once.

Then they pull back just enough to kiss my cheek—soft, warm, lingering longer than a "just friends" kiss should. But not asking anything from me either. Safe. Familiar. Gentle.

It feels like more.

It feels like nothing I have a name for.

"I told you I'd land it," they grin, breathless.

"You did," I say, smiling like an idiot. "You were incredible."

They blush, a soft pink that makes my heart do slow flips and loop their arm through mine like it's always belonged there.

I still don't know what it means.

But I know it means something.

We spend the rest of the afternoon together, we wander around the rink lobby, stealing free samples of cocoa mix from a display like criminals, like I don't work here. Eventually we find Esme near the skate rental counter.

There's no tension. No shadow of old fights. Esme gives Jada a tiny salute. Jada gives her a polite nod. It's awkward, sure, but...not bad. Not world-ending.

Esme even laughs when Jada trips over her own skate guard, nearly taking out a vending machine.

"You are a mess," Esme groans.

"Oh please, I'm adorable," Jada corrects, laughing.

I just shake my head. "Both can be true."

It's easy. The kind of easy I forgot life could be.

.✳❄*.❄.*❄*✳.*

Later, I make my way into town alone, half-floating through the day like my body's made of slightly warmer air.

I duck into the Ralph's Burger Place nearby for a sandwich and freeze.

Viviana is sitting in the corner with a whole crowd of friends—laughing, hair shiny, eyes bright in that way she used to look at me when life was still soft.

They're passing a basket of fries back and forth, teasing each other, nudging shoulders. She's glowing. Effortless.

And I hate it.

I hate the sharp twist in my ribs, the jealousy, the ache.

But then—she turns. Just slightly. And I see something in her expression I wasn't ready for.

She looks...good.

Better.

Fine, even.

Like she got her pieces back in a way I still haven't.

And it hits me like cold lake water:

Why does it hurt that she's happy?

I leave without ordering. The door jingles behind me, too cheerful for the way my chest feels.

I end up at the park without meaning to. The cold air bites at my face, but my headphones play something steady and low, a quiet that fills the empty parts of my brain.

I sit on a bench and watch the trees sway, the snow drift in lazy spirals.

"She changed," I say aloud, breath fogging. *I can see that now.*

My voice is barely above a whisper.

And I just... hate that she waited until after I was gone.

The wind doesn't offer an answer. It just moves.

I lean back, close my eyes. For a long minute, I let the ache burn through without fighting it.

I don't forgive her. Not yet. Maybe not ever.

But, I let go of the version of her I'd been clutching like a wound. I let go of the idea that she's still the person who broke me.

She's someone else now.

And so am I.

The music keeps playing. The sky keeps breathing.

And I stay on that bench until the sun dips low and the cold starts kissing my fingertips. I'm thinking about Jada's arms around me, the sting in my palms, the way life is slowly, painfully, stitching itself back together.

Not neat.

Not perfect.

But real.

chapter twenty-six

My mom walks beside me on the icy sidewalk, like she's afraid I'll vanish if she blinks. She's trying to play it cool, but every few steps she adjusts her scarf or glances at me or asks if I'm cold—three times in one block.

I don't blame her. I'm nervous enough for both of us.

The Institute looks less like a sterile medical place and more like a renovated house with too many windows, but as big as The Great Wolf Lodge. The light spills out warm and soft, and when I open the front door it smells like cinnamon and tea.

Mom squeezes my arm.

"I'll be right here when you're done."

I nod, swallow, and walk inside.

And immediately stop.

Because it's...cozy.

Comfortable.

Not what I expected at all.

The lobby's got a bookshelf full of graphic novels. A few lava lamps. A couple beanbags. A framed "Welcome, Human!" sign in rainbow letters. And—oh god—is that a crocheted Appa on the couch?

Before I can register any of this, a woman steps out of one of the office rooms.

"Payton Lee?"

I turn.

She's short, with warm tan skin like she's been dipped in late-summer sunlight, wavy black hair that bounces when she moves, and bright green eyes that somehow manage to feel both sharp and soft at once.

She smiles, calm and kind and weirdly familiar.

"I'm Dr. Zoey Flores. Come on back."

Her office somehow manages to look more chaotic and comforting than the lobby. Posters line the walls—*Steven Universe*, *She-Ra*, *Avatar: The Last Airbender*, and there's even lion plushies from *Voltron*.

But the one that catches my attention is the Avatar poster right behind her chair—Aang stepping forward, all four elements swirling around him.

I blink.

Oh.

Oh no.

This is going to be a thing.

She notices my stare and grins knowingly.

"Ah, you've spotted my teaching tools."

"Teaching tools?"

"Mhm," she says, settling into her chair. "Stories give us metaphors. Metaphors can help us understand ourselves. Also—shows are fun and life is already a struggle."

I...kind of love her already.

I sit on the couch, awkward, but not as stiff as I thought I'd be.

"I saw on your website," I say, picking at a thread on my sleeve. "That you do...things a bit differently..?"

Her eyes sparkle.

"Only sometimes. And only gently. If you ever do want to try something outside the box, we'll work our way into it slowly. At your pace. It's also a lot more fun to relate real life things to things some of our favorite characters go through!" she gestures to the posters around, grinning ear to ear.

"Okay," I mumble. "Cool."

"And," she adds, leaning forward with conspiratorial delight, "contrary to common belief, I do not force anyone to rewatch every emotionally devastating moment from Avatar. Although admittedly, book two is fantastic for talking about identity crises."

I choke on a laugh. Yep. I'm in trouble.

The session is long. Longer than I expect. But not heavy in the way therapy is always portrayed in movies.

It's like...wandering.

Talking.

Pausing.

Thinking.

Letting someone actually listen for once.

She asks about my dad, and she's gentle with it. Not careful like I'm fragile—but respectful, like grief is something sacred you don't poke with a stick.

She connects things I say to characters in a way that somehow doesn't feel childish.

"When you talk about shutting down," she says. "You remind me a little of Zuko after deciding he would be better off on his own and leaving his uncle. Do you remember how Zuko tells his uncle that he has to find his way in life, which Iroh understands and decides not to stop Zuko when he goes out of the cave and, after thinking about what his uncle said, decides to travel alone?"

I stare at her.

"...Are you therapizing me with firebending right now?"

She beams.

"Yes, and it's working beautifully."

I snort.

She notices when I talk about my drum set. How my voice gets lighter even though I don't intend it to.

"You like music," she says. "And art. That's amazing! The creative parts of you are the parts that survived some of the hardest things."

"Yeah," I murmur, surprised. "I guess."

"Have you thought about reconnecting with any friends from before things got hard? Or joining a music club? Something small that could help you remember who you are outside of it all. Give you a place to let loose."

I shake my head.

"I...didn't think any of that was still an option."

"It is," she says. No hesitation. No doubt. "You deserve things that make you feel like yourself. If you want, next time we can look at some more options."

Something in my chest loosens. Just a little. But enough.

When the session ends, I don't rush out. I sit for a second, staring at the Avatar poster like it might look back and give me life advice.

Dr. Flores walks me to the lobby.

"Same time next week?" she asks.

"I... yeah. I think so."

Her smile is soft. "Good. You did a hard thing today. You should be proud of yourself."

I start towards the front door when she calls out, "And remember what Iroh said to Zuko! 'In the darkest times, hope is something you give yourself. That is the meaning of inner strength.' You got this!"

I smile back towards her as she spins back into her office, before closing the door.

I step outside where my mom is waiting, her eyes searching my face like she's trying to decode my entire emotional landscape.

"Well?" she asks.

I shrug. But it's a warm shrug.

"It was...good."

Walking toward the bistro, I pull out my phone.

My fingers hover for a second, then I type:

Hey, Elio — you free right now? I'm thinking about a tattoo. Maybe in the next few weeks if you've got space.

I stare at the message.

Then hit send.

The cold bites at my cheeks, but it feels less sharp than usual.

chapter twenty-seven

The rink is colder today, the kind of cold that sneaks up your sleeves even if you swear you're dressed properly. I lace up my skates and step onto the ice just as Jada finishes another warm-up lap, blades slicing clean lines behind them.

"Ready for round two?" they call out, breath fogging in the air.

I nod, even though my stomach is doing a nervous cartwheel routine all on its own.

They take off again, building speed, arms tight, posture sharp. I watch them tuck in, spin, jump—

Double axel. Nailed. Perfect.

They skate to the boards where I'm standing, cheeks pink with pride. "Okay," they say breathlessly. "You know what's next."

"Yeah," I say. "And I hate it."

Jada laughs, light and fearless. "Practice makes progress."

"I know," I mutter, "but falling makes concussions."

She nudges my shoulder with hers. "Come on. I'll be fine. I've got this."

I want to argue, but her confidence wraps around me like a warm jacket. So I nod and step onto the ice with her this time, keeping a safe distance but close enough that she knows I'm there.

For the next hour, it's a cycle:

She tries.

She falls.

She gets up.

She tries again.

Sometimes he slams into the ice hard enough that I wince from across the rink. Sometimes he misses the timing completely. But every time, Jada gets up laughing, brushing frost off his leggings like failure is just...snow.

And then, finally—

He lands it.

A shaky, imperfect, beautiful triple that has me shouting like he just won the whole competition.

Before I can even react properly, Jada skates full-speed at me and throws their arms around my neck. I brace for impact, my shins already planning their funeral—but I stay upright.

Not only that, but I'm able to lift them a little, spinning once, the both of us breathless and grinning.

"That was amazing!" I laugh.

She's glowing. Like actually glowing. Like someone turned a dimmer switch for the rest of the world and decided she deserved full brightness.

We make it to the bleachers, still buzzing. I grab the little ice pack I always bring now—because it's Jada, and they're always one enthusiastic jump away from a bruise—and hand it to them.

"Thanks," they murmur, pressing it to their knee.

We sit there, legs swinging, breath settling. And before I can overthink it, I say:

"I've been thinking about talking to Viviana."

She glances at me, surprised but not judgmental. "You want to?"

"I—I think I should."

The words roll out faster now, like they've been itching under my ribs.

"You were right. I can't let all of this...everything she did...just keep controlling me. I'm tired of being scared of a person who's not even in my life anymore."

Jada nods softly. "I'll support you. Whatever you choose."

"That's the thing," I say. "I want to choose something. Instead of letting it haunt me."

She touches my arm, her palm light and grounding. "Then choose. And start where you can."

So I pull out my phone. Scroll to my contacts. My thumb hesitates over the long-buried name.

Viviana González.

Blocked.

She's been blocked so long that her last name is outdated.

It feels like a stone lodged in my throat.

But Jada is right here. Warm. Steady. Quietly brave in all the ways I'm not.

So I exhale and tap the screen.

Unblock.

The screen does its little confirmation buzz, and something in my chest shifts—not relief, exactly. But movement.

A beginning.

chapter twenty-eight

Therapy again. Week...what, four? Five? I've lost count. All I know is that Dr. Flores is sitting across from me, legs crossed, notebook perched on her knee like it's listening just as hard as she is.

"And that," she says, tapping her pen. "Is why your old therapist clearly had no idea what he was doing. You're demonstrating progress simply by acknowledging patterns he never addressed."

I can't help the tiny laugh that sneaks out. "Yeah, I figured something was off when he told me to think 'positive thoughts' after my anxiety attack."

She snorts. Actually snorts. "Please don't remind me. Anyway." She flips a page. "Before we wrap up, any new developments since last session?"

I pick at the sleeve of my hoodie. My throat goes tight. "I...yeah. I unblocked Viviana."

Her eyebrows lift. "That sounds significant."

"It's...whatever." I shrug. "She doesn't know she's unblocked. I mean—maybe she does, because I keep getting notifications. From her number. But I haven't read any of them."

"You delete them?"

"Almost instantly."

A beat.

"But I've been tempted. Every time."

She watches me, kind but sharp. The perfect combination of therapist and cartoon-wizard. "Why tempted?"

"I—I don't know..."

She gives me the look. The same one she gave when I tried pretending sleep deprivation wasn't affecting me.

"I think you do."

I exhale. Hard. "I mean...I wanna know what she's been texting me about."

"But?"

"But—" My leg bounces. My stomach flips. "I don't know. It's dumb."

"Not dumb."

"Fine. Stupid."

"No. Payton..." Her voice softens in a way that makes my chest ache. "Do you know why you've held onto this for so long?"

"Well, yea." I say, a little too fast. "She ruined my chances at MIT. She literally cut the strings."

"Okay. So why do you care what's in those messages?"

"I—"

Her silence is louder than a shout.

She leans forward. "Do you think, maybe, there could be something you've wanted to hear in them?"

The air leaves my lungs. My mouth opens—then shuts. Like if I speak, everything I've stuffed down for two years will come spilling out across her office floor.

She checks the clock. "We're almost out of time."

My stomach drops.

"But I have a homework assignment for you."

"Okay..." I brace myself.

"I want you to text her."

I stare. Blink. "W-what? No, what? Text—her?"

"You don't have to do it today," she says calmly. "Or even tomorrow. But I want you to try typing something before our next session."

"And if I can't?"

"Then that's okay. We'll try again another time."

Relief floods me.

"That doesn't mean you can procrastinate it."

Relief immediately dries up like a puddle in July. "Right. Yeah. Got it."

Her timer goes off. She waves, warm and casual, like she didn't just assign me the psychological equivalent of walking into a haunted house blindfolded.

I wave back and step out into the hallway.

*.❄ * ❄ *. ❄ .* ❄ * ❄ .*

I'm halfway down the block when her assignment starts swirling around my brain.

Text Viviana.

Like actually text her.

Like words. To her face. Well—phone.

She can't be serious...right?

I walk into the bistro to grab a coffee and freeze.

Viviana. Working the counter. Laughing with a coworker.

Thursday. Why Thursday? Why now?

Nope. No thank you. Not today.

I back out so fast I almost knock into a table and walk straight down the street, pulling my phone out.

I text Elio: omw

If I'm going to have a crisis, I'd rather do it while someone stabs ink into my skin.

*. ❄ * ❄ *. ❄ .* ❄ * ❄ .*

Madeline's is like stepping into a time machine set to 1973 and adjusted for maximum bisexual lighting. Warm amber lamps, plants everywhere, records on the walls, incense that smells like cedar and art students.

Cozy. Weirdly cozy.

At the front desk sits a girl with red-braided hair so long it looks like a weapon of mass destruction. Ink covers her arms in flowers and tiny birds. Silver piercings glint across her ears. Lip ring. Nose stud. She looks like she stepped out of a Pinterest board.

She glances up, neutral expression—then breaks into a huge grin.

"Hi! Welcome in! I'm Madeline. Got an appointment today?"

"Uh—yeah." I clear my throat. "I'm here for Elio? I'm Payton."

"Oh! One sec."

She whips her chair around and hollers down the hallway:

"ELIO! YOUR KID IS HERE!"

I blink. "Kid?"

She turns back to me, laughing. "I've heard so much about you. It's nice to finally put a face to the name. He'll meet you right here."

She points at an empty table like it's a throne. "Have fun!"

Elio finally shows up, bouncing on the balls of his feet like a caffeinated golden retriever.

"Sooo," he grins, rubbing his hands together, "what are we thinking?"

I pull out my phone and show him Austin's drawing—a cassette tape wrapped in flowers, the word memories scribbled across it.

"Austin drew it a while ago," I say. "And I think it's perfect."

Elio whistles. "Dude. This is sick." He sends it to his tablet. "Gimme five minutes to draw this up."

He sketches, prints, preps the stencil.

I show him where I want it on my calf. He nods. Gloves snap on. The machine buzzes.

Halfway through, I swallow hard. "Hey, can I ask you something?"

"Shoot."

"You know how I'm in therapy?"

"Yeah?"

"She wants me to text Viviana."

He doesn't react dramatically. Doesn't gasp. Just shrugs. "Okay. What about it?"

"You don't think that's crazy?"

"Not really." He gets a wipe. "I mean, it's been almost two years now."

I scoff. "So what are you saying?"

He sighs. "I'm saying what we've all been thinking. You can't let this control your life anymore. So text her. Might help both of you."

"You really think so?"

"Yes. Now *shh*. I'm doing tiny lines."

I roll my eyes and stare at the ceiling, slipping one earbud in while he tattoos the rest of the cassette.

My thoughts keep circling the same drain.

Viviana.

Her messages.

Whatever she's trying to say...I'm scared to hear.

*. ❄ * ❅ *. ❆ .* ❅ * ❄ .*

By the time I get home, my calf is wrapped, sore, and kinda throbbing like a bass drum. I lie on my bed in the dark, ceiling glowing with faint fairy lights, notes app open.

The keyboard blinks at me.

Mocking me.

What would I even say?

After ten minutes of getting nowhere, I drop my arms to my sides and groan at the ceiling.

My phone buzzes.

Jada.

Goodnight <3

I smile without meaning to. I text back:

night :)

When I close the chat, I see it.

Viviana's name.

Typing bubble. Disappear.

Typing again.

Disappear.

I hover. Heart pounding. Then—

A message pops up.

I miss you.

My breath catches. I sit up so fast my newly tattooed leg screams at me.

She types again. Stops.

I start typing. Stop.

Start again. She goes silent.

And I send it:

Can we talk?

quarter 4

"We have to live bravely in order to truly feel alive"

- Taylor Swift

chapter twenty-nine

Honestly, I wasn't expecting the message to even send. My thumb had hovered over the little blue arrow for a full minute like it was a detonator and I was about to blow up whatever fragile progress I'd made in life lately.

But the message went through.

And she answered.

And then—somehow she said yes.

Which is why I was here, sitting in the bistro at ten at night like someone waiting for a job interview they were forced to apply for. I'd picked the same table I always gravitated toward, probably because routine felt safer than the hundred spiraling thoughts pinballing in my brain.

My coffee sat in front of me, half-cold in a paper to-go cup, the surface rippling slightly every time my leg bounced. The place was too quiet. Too still. In the daytime, the bistro hummed with clattering mugs and overlapping voices and the soft hiss of the espresso machine. Now? Now it was just wood and shadows and the distant hum of a refrigerator in the back.

The air felt thick, like it was waiting with me.

I held the cup between my hands, letting the warmth seep into my palms while my mind did its usual Olympic-level catastrophizing.

She's going to be angry.

She's going to pretend she's not.

She's going to pretend everything's fine.

She's going to cry.

I'm going to cry.

I am not crying in this bistro. I refuse.

I nearly spilled the coffee when the back lights clicked off—one, two, three—in a chain, leaving the kitchen in darkness. Only the front pendant lamps remained, casting this warm but weirdly claustrophobic glow over everything.

It felt like the walls leaned in.

I pressed a thumb into the tiny chip in the table's varnish, worrying the edge of it because my hands couldn't figure out how to be still.

Viviana tossed her apron onto the counter top, stretching her shoulders like closing had been a full workout. When she turned toward me, the expression on her face wasn't what I expected. It wasn't cold. It wasn't guarded. It wasn't even awkward.

It was...fragile. A weak smile held together with frayed thread.

"Shall we?" she said softly.

I nodded. My throat was too tight for words anyway. Standing made it worse. My legs felt like wet noodles, and my fingers automatically found my rings, spinning them, sliding them, adjusting them like my life depended on it.

We stepped outside into the quiet, biting cold. The air felt cleaner than the bistro's stale, over-coffee'd humidity, but it didn't settle me.

We walked.

Neither of us said anything. Our footsteps were loud against the pavement, echoing off the empty storefronts. The streetlights glowed through the bare winter branches overhead, throwing spindly shadows across the sidewalk.

A couple blocks later, Sherlock Park came into view, dimly lit, mostly empty except for a jogger in the distance and two teens holding hands by the baseball field. The pond was iced over, reflecting the lights in cracked, broken pieces.

Viviana shoved her hands into her coat pockets. That surprised me. She used to walk like she was ready to sprint into any conversation, any moment, any disaster. Now she looked small. Tired. Heavy.

The silence pressed on us until it hurt.

"So—um…" she started.

"You never stopped texting," I blurted. The words came out sharper than I meant. "Why?"

She froze just enough that I caught the tension ripple through her shoulders. Her breath puffed in the cold, uneven.

"I—" She tried again. "I mean... you have the messages, right...?"

"No."

"Oh." Her voice shrank. "Oh."

Another silence. This one worse.

"There was... a lot of stuff that happened back then," she said quietly. Her eyes flickered to the frozen pond, then back to the ground. "And I—" Her breath hitched. "I didn't know how to handle it all."

We reached the little wooden bridge in the center of the park. She drifted toward it automatically, like muscle memory guided her more than thought. Her hand slid along the railing, fingertips brushing the frost-dusted wood.

I followed, keeping a careful few steps between us.

"I know what you're gonna say," she whispered, voice floating up into the dark like it was afraid to exist. "How could I have done that? Stayed away for months."

She let out a shaky laugh—small, bitter.

"I had no right to be angry at you for so long," she said. "There's nothing that excuses what I did."

I stepped onto the middle of the bridge with her. She still didn't look at me. Instead, she tightened her grip on the railing, knuckles white, breath unsteady.

"But I also need you to understand..." She swallowed. "I know I left you in the dark. About everything. I thought you wouldn't understand."

I exhaled sharply. Not angry, just...tired. Tired in a way I hadn't let myself recognize until right now.

"It was wrong," she said. Her voice cracked. "I see that now. And I'm—"

She paused, breath shaking.

"I'm so sorry."

And there it was.

Those three stupid little words that shouldn't have mattered, that shouldn't have had the power to unravel something inside my chest, but they did. They landed in a place I'd boarded up, layered over, ignored for years.

She went quiet again. Really quiet.

"I know that won't change anything," she whispered. "Or turn back time. But I need you to know...even if you don't care, or don't want to forgive me."

She laughed, soft and miserable. "I wouldn't blame you. I ruined your whole future."

The words collapsed into a whisper.

"Payton..." She curled her fingers tighter around the railing. "Aren't you going to say anything...?"

I looked at her. Really looked. At her red nose, her trembling lip, her eyes finally lifting to mine. She looked scared. Not of me. Not of the past.

Scared of the truth.

"What...? What's the face...?" she asked nervously.

"I just—" I started, my voice breaking embarrassingly fast. "I never thought that—"

I sighed, breath fogging the air.

"Thank you," I whispered.

Her lips parted, like she hadn't expected that answer at all.

"Also—I found this in the elevator a few months ago...figured you might want it back." I said, pulling her gold ring with the orange gem out of my pocket.

She took it from me, careful not to drop it, unsure if it was real. She stared at it for a bit before pocketing it, wiping her eye with her pointer finger.

Silence fell again, but this time it was different. It wasn't suffocating. It wasn't sharp. It was...quiet. Soft. Almost peaceful.

Then my mouth betrayed me again. "I'm—uh—I'm sorry about the formal," I blurted out. Because apparently I am committed to ruining every emotionally charged moment with abrupt confessions.

She blinked fast. "You—you don't have to...There's nothing to apologize for."

"Sienna told me they changed the date." I kept my voice gentle.

Viviana's posture shifted. Her shoulders hitched, and she clenched her fists like she was bracing for impact.

"Even so," she murmured, staring at the ice below. "I had no right to ask you for anything. And you would've had every right not to show. And I shouldn't have...hurt you like that."

Her voice splintered, cracking like the ice below us.

"And I—" she exhaled sharply, "I know you don't have to forgive me. But...can we try again...?"

She said it so quietly I almost missed it. Not try again romantically or like nothing happened.

Try again as people. As human beings who used to matter to each other.

I didn't know the right words. I didn't trust myself to speak at all, honestly. My throat felt like it had closed up, and the cold suddenly stung my eyes.

I stayed silent for too long.

Her shoulders fell. She started to step back from me, from the railing, from the conversation entirely.

Instinct moved faster than thought.

I reached out, gently looping an arm around her in a small, hesitant side hug—a gesture so soft it felt like asking a question.

"Yeah," I whispered.

Her breath hitched, just once.

And for the first time in almost two years, we stood there. Not enemies, not strangers, just two people finally telling each other the truth.

chapter thirty

The rink always looks colder when you're walking toward it instead of skating on it.

The overhead lights hum, the boards gleam just enough to catch every reflection, and the whole place has that faint, metallic chill that sneaks down your neck. My breath fogs as I push through the door, and for a second I wonder if the cold is going to seize my lungs before I even lace up.

Jada's already out there, doing slow circles like she's testing the ice for cracks. The girl never actually waits patiently she just looks like she does. She notices me the second my skate blades hit the ice.

"There he is," she calls, skating backward toward me with her hands behind her back, like a show-off. "Didn't think you were actually gonna make it."

"Yeah, right," I mutter, tightening my gloves. "Missing practice would mean hearing you complain for the next three days."

She smirks. "You say that like I wouldn't do that anyway."

I step onto the ice fully. It bites under my blades, grounding. My body instantly falls back into place, like someone cracked my spine and all the pieces slid back where they were supposed to be. Jada watches my face for a beat, and she must see something, because the teasing drops.

"You good?" she asks quietly.

It hangs there, that question. After everything—the fight with Viviana, the blow-up at home, the apologies that weren't easy or pretty—I'm still a little raw. My chest isn't as heavy, but there's...space now. Unsteady space.

I start skating slow laps with her at my side. "Yeah," I say. "Kinda. Mostly."

She bumps my shoulder lightly with hers. "I talked to Viviana," she says after a moment. "She said things went...well."

I huff a laugh. "Yeah, that's one way to put it."

"She didn't tell me everything," Jada adds quickly. "She said it wasn't her story to tell. Which, like... wow, growth."

I snort. "She's capable of growth. Who knew."

But then the humor fades, because I know where this is going. And I know Jada—if there's even a hint of something off about me, they'll poke at it like it's a bear.

"So," they say, sliding right into it, "you gonna talk about it?"

"Maybe," I say, dragging out the word. "Give me a minute to pretend I'm mysterious and closed-off."

"You're about as mysterious as a traffic cone." They laugh.

"Rude."

"But true."

We skate in silence for a bit. Not awkward, Jada doesn't do awkward, and I think I'm finally realizing I don't have to, either. The ice scrapes under us, echoing, rhythmic. My muscles warm. My lungs feel clearer.

Eventually, I exhale. "I talked to my mom," I say, voice low. "Really talked. About that night. About... everything."

Jada nods. "You mean...just that night or—"

They don't even have to specify.

"Yeah," I say. "Everything."

They wait. That's the part they're best at...not forcing anything...at least when it matters.

"It got bad," I admit. "Like, yelling. And then not yelling. More like...breaking. For both of us."

They're eyebrows pinch a little, but they stay quiet.

"I told her why I keep pretending everything's fine," I continue. "Why I keep thinking—" I swallow. My throat tightens just remembering. "Why I keep thinking it was all on me. Because it was my fault."

Jada's breath fogs in front of him. "Payton..."

"I know. I know it's not actually all my fault. I know that up here." I tap my temple with my glove. "But knowing something isn't the same as believing it."

"And your mom?" he asks.

I let out a shaky breath. "She said she was scared. That she hated not knowing how to help. That she didn't realize how much I was carrying because I've always been 'the strong one'." I make air quotes. "Like that's even a real job."

"It kinda is," Jada says softly. "And it kinda sucks."

"Yeah. She cried. I cried. It was a whole thing."

"Whoa—you cried? Like, actual tears? Out your actual eyes?"

"Shut up."

He grins. "I'm proud of you."

The words hit harder than they should. I dig my toe pick into the ice. "She wanted me to start therapy. And I did."

"You actually said yes? No sarcasm?"

"I mean, I did make a joke first."

"Of course you did."

He grabs my sleeve and pulls me toward center ice, where the overhead lights are brightest. "So what'd Viv say about all this?"

I drag a hand through my hair. "That she was worried. Annoyed, but worried. Mostly annoyed."

"Fair."

"And she apologized. And then demanded I stop pretending I'm fine just to keep everyone else from worrying."

Jada snorts.

"She wasn't wrong," I admit.

"I know she wasn't wrong," Jada says. "You've got this whole hero complex going on."

"It's not a hero complex." I shake my head. "It's just—someone had to keep things moving. Someone had to be okay."

"And you picked yourself," she says. "Every time."

"Yeah."

She glides backward, studying me carefully. Thinking before saying, "So...about the dance."

I groan. "Wow, subtle."

"What? I let you spill your guts first. That's generous."

"You're terrible."

"And yet you keep hanging out with me." She gives me a pointed look. "So. Are you going or not?"

"I didn't say I wasn't going."

"You didn't say you were."

I sigh, pushing off into a smooth glide. "Look...after everything that's happened? I think I *need* something normal."

"So...that's a yes?" she asks, eyes shining with amusement and maybe a little hope.

I shrug, but it's half-smile, half-surrender. "Yeah. Fine. Yes."

Jada lets out a joyful scream and almost wipes out. "Seriously?! Dude, I've been asking for like ever—"

"It has not been that long."

"Emotionally it has."

I laugh for real—the kind that scrapes something loose in my chest. "You're ridiculous."

"And you're going to look amazing in dance-appropriate clothing."

"I'm regretting this already."

"Nope! No take-backs!"

She loops around me, fast and sharp, leaving a crescent of shaved ice in her wake. "Payton's going to the dance!" she sings, echoing across the rink.

I chase her across the ice, the cold air slicing past my face, my heart lighter than it's been in months. I let myself stop carrying everything. Just skate. Just breathe. I'm actually getting really good at this.

And it feels good. Not perfect, not fixed, but good enough to believe I might actually be okay.

Eventually.

chapter thirty-one

By the time I push open the door to the Bistro, the midday sun is still slanting warm across the tile floor, catching on the glass jars of tea and the big chalkboard menu that's permanently smudged no matter how many times someone wipes it down.

The place smells like strawberries, vanilla syrup, and something cinnamon-adjacent. Spring is starting to integrate itself back into our lives. It's half-full with a few college kids on laptops, an older couple sharing a muffin, someone at the bar scribbling in a notebook.

But I'm not here for all of that.

It's been a few weeks since Viviana and I talked and, needless to say, things have been ok.

Jada spots me first. She waves both arms like she's trying to flag down a rescue plane. "Payton! We got the table!"

Viviana's sitting sideways in the seat, one leg tucked under her, hair in two messy buns. Her nails are black with sharp little silver stars painted on them. Esme is next to her, typing aggressively on her computer like the device owes her money.

I slide in next to Jada.

"Didn't know you were off today," I say to Viviana.

She shrugs. "Night shift at the studio. Slinging ink til' midnight and I *refuse* to work a double. Let this place burn without me."

Esme pats her shoulder. "It would collapse in five minutes."

"Exactly," she says proudly.

"Slinging ink?" Jada repeats. "Do you even sleep?"

"Occasionally," Viviana says. "Like a bat."

Vinny drops off four drinks—Jada's iced lavender latte, Esme's raspberry iced matcha with cold foam, my usual matcha, and Viviana's black coffee that smells like it could melt paint.

"So," Jada says, leaning forward, "competition. Update."

Viviana props her chin in her hand. "Are you ready?"

"I think so...I'm getting really good at that axel."

"At least it doesn't look chaotic anymore." I laugh.

"Speaking of chaotic," Jada says, turning to Viviana. "You're still working both jobs? Why?"

She shrugs like it's no big deal. "Yeah. Bistro during the day, the studio at night. Bills exist. Also I'm building my portfolio, and the night crowd gives better tips."

"What about your majors?" Jada says. "How are you even handling two?"

Viviana takes a long sip of coffee. "Psychology and film. One is for my brain, the other is for my soul."

"And the tattoos?" I ask.

"For my wallet," she deadpans.

We all laugh.

Esme stretches her fingers like she's preparing to conduct a symphony. "I cannot believe you balance all that. I'm drowning in my biochem homework. This master's program and grading at least one-hundred versions of the same test is killing me. I do not get paid enough." She slumps down into her chair staring at the screen. Viviana puts her arm around her, kissing her forehead.

"You get paid for tutoring too," Jada reminds her.

"That barely counts," Esme mutters. "Anyway—Payton?"

I look up. "What?"

"What do you do? You never talk about school," Esme says. "Ever."

I see Viviana tense slightly. "There's not much to talk about," I say. "I'm just working on getting my associate's. I'm just trying not to fail history."

"You're doing great," Jada says, nudging me with her shoulder.

Viviana tilts her head. "You ever think about transferring? After the associate's?"

I blink. That's...not a question I've ever let myself consider. "I mean...I don't know," I say. "I haven't really thought that far. I'm kinda just...surviving semester by semester."

Viviana's eyebrows pull together gently. "You could. If you wanted. You're smart enough."

Heat creeps up my neck. "Thanks."

*.❅ * ❆ *. ❇ .* ❆ * ❅ .*

We wandered to the park together, the four of us spilling out of the Bistro like we were still carrying the warmth of it. The air had cooled; dusk unfurled slow and purple across the sky, staining everything with that hour-before-night glow. The lamps along the trail

294

flickered on one by one, each a soft yellow halo over the path.

Esme and Jada drifted ahead, naturally pairing off, Esme's hand looping around Jada's wrist as she tugged her toward the bridge. They paused halfway across it, framed by the water below, laughing as Jada tried to get the perfect picture of the fading sun.

Which left me and Viviana trailing behind.

She kicked a pebble down the path. "They're cute," she said, nodding toward the two of them on the bridge.

"Yeah." The word slipped out easily. Maybe too easy. "So, you and Esme huh?"

She huffed. "Yea...she's amazing."

I laughed, shoving my hands into my pockets. "You—uhm...you look good together. It—it makes sense."

She slowed, just a bit, like she was trying to catch a shift in the wind. "Thanks," she said quietly. "We're...trying."

There was something softer in her voice. Something I wasn't sure I was allowed to ask about. So I didn't. But the quiet settled between us, not uncomfortable, but fragile enough to notice.

We reached the start of the bridge, leaning against the wooden rail while Esme snapped pictures and Jada pretended to pose, then messed it up on purpose. Viviana smiled at them, and then at me, nudging my shoulder with hers.

"So," she said.

"What?"

"You know," she said, drawing out the vowels.

"I have no idea what you're talking about."

She sighed dramatically, like she was exhausted. "You really don't see it?"

I blinked. "See what?"

She turned to face me fully, folding her arms. "You like her."

My stomach dropped so fast I felt it hit the ground. "Wh—I—what? No! I—absolutely not." My voice cracked like I was thirteen again and my dignity dissolved on the spot.

She raised an eyebrow.

"I don't—I don't like her like that...we're just friends," I muttered, staring very hard at a lamp post.

"You do," she said simply. "And it's not subtle."

"I really don't."

"You really do."

I groaned. "Come on."

She didn't let up. "Payton, you look at her like you're trying not to breathe too loud. And you hover near her like she's gonna disappear if you don't. And when she smiles at you? You get that stupid soft look in your eyes."

"I do not have soft eyes."

"You do! I would know," she said, laughing under her breath. "It's cute."

Heat rushed up my neck. "Look, whatever you think I'm feeling—I'm not."

"Oh, I'm sorry. I thought we said we'd stop lying to each other. I must've heard you wrong." she laughed.

I swallowed hard. The world felt too still for a second—even the water beneath the bridge held its breath.

"I don't think I..." I started. Then stopped. "I don't know."

Her expression softened. All the teasing slipped into something honest. "It's okay not to know," she said quietly. "Just...don't lie to yourself because it's easier."

Something in my chest twisted, not painful, just...strange. Like a door I'd boarded up rattled from the inside.

"Hey!" Jada called from the middle of the bridge. "Viv! Payt! Get over here! The sky looks like cotton candy!"

Viviana grinned. "Saved by the pink clouds."

As we walked to join them, I tried to ignore the warmth creeping under my ribs. Tried to ignore the part of me whispering that maybe—just maybe—she wasn't wrong.

I didn't like her.

...Right?

chapter thirty-two

The car still smells like sweat and pine-tar resin.

It's Austin's fault, obviously.

Austin climbs into the back seat with all the subtlety of a collapsing building, tossing his backpack down and immediately kicking off his shoes like we're not in a shared space. Mom gives him *That Look*—the one that says try me—and he puts them back on with a groan.

And then we're off.

I sit passenger-side now. It's the one place where my heartbeat doesn't crawl up my throat, where the seatbelt doesn't feel like a rope around my chest. I don't drive. Not yet. Not again.

But I'm not panicking, either.

The world passes by the windows in soft blurs. Familiar houses, trees I could draw from memory, the road I used to speed down without thinking. My fingers automatically find the seam of the seat, tracing it. It keeps me grounded.

But I'm still somewhere else.

Vivianas's voice echoes.

You've never thought about transferring?

You could. If you wanted. You're smart enough.

Why not try?

Because.

Because I don't get things like that.

Because I'm not supposed to want more than what I've already taken away.

Because college, real college? That costs money. And I've been saving for Austin. And Mom still gets overwhelmed with Millie's meltdowns. She's not even a year old yet. Mom needs help.

And someone has to be around. Someone responsible.

Someone like me.

I stare at my reflection in the passenger window—the tired eyes, the faint bruise-colored smudges from too many late nights. I look older than I actually am.

"You're quiet," Mom says.

Her tone is soft. It makes my chest tighten.

"I'm always quiet."

She glances over from the driver's seat. "What's going on in that head?"

I shrug, watching the trees flick past. "Just...stuff."

"Payton."

There's a whole lecture in the way she says my name. No judgment, just that gentle persistence Mom's perfected.

I take a breath.

"Well...Viviana asked me something."

Her eyebrows lift. "Viviana?"

"Yeah."

"What did she say?"

I pick at my thumbnail. The words scrape their way up my throat. "She asked if I was going to transfer after I finish my associates."

Mom is quiet for a moment. Just...waiting.

"And?"

"I never thought about it," I mutter. "Like—ever. I don't know. I just assumed I'd stay here, or...work, or..." I wave my hand, feeling stupid. "I don't wanna mess things up. I've been saving for Austin. And you need help with Millie, and—"

"Payton," Mom says, and it's soft but firm. "Sweetheart, look at me."

I do.

And she looks at me like she's seeing someone she didn't know standing right in front of her.

"You are allowed to think about your own future."

My throat closes. "But—"

"You wouldn't ruin anything," she says, sharper now. "And you don't owe the world some kind of lifelong repayment. You get to have dreams."

The breath shudders out of me.

Mom continues, "If you want to transfer, we will figure it out. If you want to be done after your associates, we'll figure that out too. But you don't have to make yourself small because of what happened."

There it is again, this strange, disarming softness in my chest. Like my ribs loosened.

"But Austin—"

"Is fine," she says. "And will continue to be fine."

"And Millie—"

"Has me and Ms. Dahlia next-door in her life, not just you."

"But you—"

She reaches over, squeezing my shoulder. "Need you to be happy more than I need anything else."

...Oh.

Well.

That sentence rearranges something in me.

I turn back to the window, blinking fast. Talking felt like tipping over a bucket. Everything spilling out at once. Everything suddenly too real.

Mom doesn't push. She just turns on the radio. Austin groans. Millie babbles along off-key. Mom taps the steering wheel, pretending none of us are tone-deaf.

And somehow, the car doesn't feel like a trap.

It feels like a place I'm allowed to breathe.

A few streets later, Mom pulls into a parking lot, and I don't even need to look to know where we are.

Bluey's.

The electric-blue neon sign buzzes above the windows. It hasn't changed since I was little, same cartoon dog mascot, same striped awning, same chalkboard sign with misspelled menu items.

"This was your favorite," Mom says as she puts the car in park.

She doesn't say *I thought you deserved something good.*

She doesn't have to.

Austin cheers. Millie kicks her feet. I let out a laugh I didn't expect.

And walking into Bluey's, the cold air, the smell of waffle cones, the rainbow of scoops in the freezer, the stupid "PUP SCOOP!" kid size cup sign. It feels like stepping into one of the few places time hasn't managed to ruin.

Maybe Viv is right.

Maybe Mom is right.

Maybe wanting more isn't a crime.

I'm not sure yet.

chapter thirty-three

I get to the rink a little early, mostly because sitting at home with my thoughts swirling around was making me antsy.

The place is colder than usual, but still has that familiar bite that seeps through your sleeves and makes your breath show. Jada's already out on the ice doing slow laps, warming up their legs, the rhythm of their skates scraping clean lines into the surface.

They spot me and wave, gliding over with that mix of excitement and nerves that's become their baseline these days. "Final practice," they say, bouncing once on their toe pick like it's a springboard. There's this determined look in their eyes, the kind you only get when you've spent weeks chasing something until your body memorizes it better than your brain does.

I lean on the boards. "Last one before the competition," I say. "Feeling ready?"

They shrug, but it doesn't hide the smile tugging at their mouth. "I think I've got the triple pretty solid now."

She pushes off and heads toward the far end of the rink. I watch her go through her warm-up jumps, the simpler ones she can do practically in her sleep. I've seen her fall enough times to know the exact sound her blades make when she's off balance, but right now everything sounds clean and controlled. When she finally goes for the triple axel, she rotates fast, lands a little heavy, but she lands. The thud echoes, and she exhales in a way that says she didn't entirely believe it until just now.

"That was solid," I call out. I don't raise my voice often, but she earned it.

She skates back to me, cheeks flushed from the cold and the adrenaline. "Round one was smooth," she says. "And if I hit that in Riverside, I just might place!"

I nod, trying to ignore the flick of nerves in my stomach. Riverside? I knew it was coming up, but hearing it out loud makes the distance feel real. "Where exactly is it?" I ask, making sure I was hearing correctly.

"Next town over?" she says, unlacing her gloves and flexing her hands. "About an hour by car. Three hours or so if someone walked it, but don't. Like—don't ever walk the highway." Her eyes widen in emphasis. "I'm taking a bus with the other competitors. They're picking us up from here."

I swallow. I can practically feel my pulse in my neck. Buses. Highways. Fast cars. She says it so casually because to her it is casual. To me it's...not. But that's not her problem, and I'm not about to make her proud moment about my stupid hang-ups.

"I'll be there," I say. I hope it comes out confident. It mostly does.

He plants the butt of his skate against the wall and looks at me like he's trying to read something under the surface. "Your mom can give you a ride?"

"I—yeah. Yeah, she can." I look down at my own skates. "I'll ask her tonight."

He taps my arm with the end of his glove. "Good. It—It means a lot to me that you're coming."

I don't know how to respond to that without sounding weird, so I just nod and follow him onto the ice. This part still feels strange sometimes—me skating next to him—but I'm getting used to the wobble of it. I trail behind while he works through his routine again. Fall, push up, reset. Fall again, curse under his breath, reset. Over and over. His determination is so sharp it could cut through the boards.

By the one-hour mark, he finally nails a landing with absolutely no wobble. He screams a genuine "holy crap I did it" yell and drops into this little crouch like he's trying not to explode.

I hear myself laugh. It surprises me.

They skate straight toward me and practically throw themselves into a hug. I barely stay upright, but I do, somehow. They loop their arms around my neck, and I catch them by the waist, lifting them automatically, enough that her blades leave the ice for a second. They're lighter than I thought. Or maybe I'm stronger than I give myself credit for.

When we pull apart, they're grinning at me like they just won the lottery. "Finals, Payton. I'm going to the finals."

"Yeah," I say. "You are."

She leads us to the bleachers once practice wraps. The ice machine comes out behind us, loud and slow, scraping away all our skid marks. I grab some ice from the front desk and pass it to her for her knee—she always pretends it doesn't hurt, but she takes the ice anyway.

We sit there for a minute, both catching our breath. The rink feels strangely quiet without her jumps echoing off the walls.

"So..." I start, staring at the ice machine because it's easier than looking at him. "About earlier. What you said about Riverside."

She hums in acknowledgment.

"I don't know," I admit. "I've been thinking about it and knowing for sure that the competition's out of town? I don't know, I'm—" I shut my mouth before I say scared. The word feels too big.

She doesn't push. She just listens, eyes steady, knee balanced under the ice pack.

"You should try," he says finally. "Not because of me or the competition or anything like that. Just...you should try for yourself."

I nod. It lands somewhere deep.

He gives me a small smile, then reaches for his bag. "Come on. You should call your mom. Tell her you need a ride to Riverside."

My phone feels heavier than usual, but I pull it out. My thumb hovers over the screen. I'm not ready yet—but later tonight, I will be.

I have to be.

chapter thirty-four

Getting ready for the dance takes me way too long for something that should've been easy. My room looks like a thrift store exploded—shirts on the bed, ties slung over the desk chair, socks I can't find matches for.

I keep telling myself I don't care that much, but I'm lying. The more I try to pretend the dance is "no big deal," the more my stomach turns like I swallowed a bag of wet marbles. I can't get my collar to sit flat. My belt keeps twisting like it's protesting. And I've redone my hair so many times my hair ties are starting to rebel out of spite.

Mom leans against the doorframe holding Millie in one arm and her blanket in the other. Millie's out cold, cheeks squished. "You look so handsome," Mom says. I mutter something noncommittal, because if I say thank you, she'll make it a whole thing.

"They're gonna love it," she adds, giving me that knowing look—the look that says she sees through me even when I'm trying my hardest to be opaque. I grab my jacket off the back of my chair and shove my arms through the sleeves before I can think too hard about it.

Mom asks as we reach the elevator door, "Want to drive? You haven't tried in a while."

My breath sticks. My chest tightens. "No," I say quickly. Her nod is soft as she helps adjust my light blue tie, no judgment, no pressure. Just acceptance.

The car ride stretches out like someone pulled the road longer. Mom fills the space and starts talking about Austin's game tomorrow, about how Millie's starting to make new little sounds, about the neighbor's weirdly aggressive cat.

I answer here and there, but my head's not fully in the conversation. It keeps drifting back to the rink, to Riverside, to Viv on the bridge, to the way everything in my life feels like puzzle pieces I've been forcing into the wrong spots. And to tonight. Mostly tonight.

When we pull into the parking lot, music bleeds faintly through the student center walls—something nostalgic, something that would've shown up in every playlist when we were seventeen. I shake my hands out before I get out of the car. Mom studies me like she wants to say something but chooses not to. "Call me when you need a ride home," she says.

"I will."

I shut the door behind me and stand there for a moment, breathing through the hum under my skin. Then I head toward the entrance.

The banner above the doors reads *A Night in the Meadow*, with painted vines curling around the letters. Inside, the hallway is lined with fake grass mats and dim lights shaped like lanterns. The whole thing looks surprisingly good. Not cheap or tacky. It was nice.

I'm late—of course I'm late—and mentally preparing myself for the possibility that the night will instantly go downhill. I step into the main ballroom, and the scene hits me like warm air: clusters of people dancing, others laughing, couples swaying, groups taking photos under the big arch of twinkle lights.

And then I see them.

Jada.

They're standing near the center of the room, talking to someone from class, and the second I really look at them, something in my brain short-circuits. Their outfit is this soft, flowing yellow— nothing dramatic, nothing loud. Just...them. Natural. Centered. Like the exact spot in the room where the light hits perfectly was chosen just for them. My breath catches. Hard.

Viv's voice slams into my memory. *It's obvious you like them.*

I swallow. Too fast. It feels like a rock drops from the back of my throat into my chest.

Jada turns their head, scanning the room, and the moment their gaze snags on me, their entire posture shifts.

He perks up slightly, eyes widening like he wasn't sure I'd show. Then he starts weaving through the crowd toward me.

The closer he gets, the more I feel like I'm sinking into the floor while being yanked toward him at the same time. I didn't think nerves could do both at once, but apparently I'm discovering all sorts of new talents today.

When he reaches me, he nudges my arm with a half-annoyed, half-relieved huff.

"I thought you bailed."

"Never," I say, and the word comes out steadier than I feel. It's quiet. Honest. *Maybe too honest.*

She softens, just a little. And for a moment, everything else—the noise, the lights, the crush of bodies—blurs away. It's just her and me standing in the middle of a staged meadow made of string lights and college-budget artistry.

The music shifts to a song with a simple pulse layered under lyrics that hit somewhere between youthful and aching. She glances toward the dance floor and then back at me.

"You're not gonna make me ask twice, right?"

"That depends on what you're asking," I counter, because apparently my default defense mechanism is sarcasm.

She rolls her eyes. "Dance with me, genius."

Oh. Right. Dancing. A thing I do not do.

But I nod. Somehow my hand finds hers. Somehow she's pulling me gently into the open space like she's been doing this with me for years.

We settle into a rhythm that isn't perfect but works—like two mismatched gears that somehow fit anyway. I'm a little stiff. They're a little too good at this, reminding me that they're a dance major and it's like...their favorite hobby.

But the more we move, the more the tension loosens. The lights sweep across their face as we sway, and I catch myself staring more than once.

Jada laughs under their breath when I stumble half a step behind the beat. "Relax," they say softly. "You're acting like someone's grading you."

"I don't want to step on you," I mutter.

"You won't."

"You don't know that."

They smirk. "I know you."

My chest tightens, not painfully, but sharply enough that I feel it.

The song shifts again, slower, more intimate. The kind of slow dance song you'd see in a coming-of-age montage. He slides one hand to my shoulder, steady and warm. My hand settles at his waist. Our foreheads almost brush.

For a few seconds, everything is still.

"See?" she murmurs. "You're fine."

I huff out a laugh. "You say that like I'm not a hazard to society."

"Only sometimes."

The room around us fades into nothing but color and murmurs. All the noises blur together like distant ocean waves. The only things that feel real are his hands, his breath, his steady presence that anchors me even though I've never asked for that from anyone.

Eventually the dance floor grows more crowded as another upbeat song kicks in. We step back, just enough to breathe. Enough to meet each other's eyes without the lights getting in the way.

Then Jada looks toward the side exit—the door that leads out to the campus garden path, the one people pretend is romantic even though it's probably only pretty after dark. She nods toward it with a small tilt of her head.

"Wanna go for a walk?" he asks, quiet but sure. Like he already knows my answer.

And before the thought is even fully formed in my mind, I say:

"Yeah."

chapter thirty-five

The air outside the auditorium is cooler than I expect, sliding over my skin like a reminder that real life exists beyond the lights and borrowed courage.

The door thunks shut behind us, muffling the last messy chords of whatever song the DJ threw on after the slow ones ended. For a second, everything feels suspended. Just me, Jada, and the soft hum of the school grounds settling into night.

I shove my hands into my pockets so I don't do something stupid or look stupid fidgeting. "The school looks...nicer at night," I say, because silence suddenly feels too loud.

They huff a laugh, nudging a stray pebble with their shoe as we start down the path. "Everything's nicer at night. It's the rule." They glance up at the stars barely visible between streetlights. "Y'know..." they start, "Logan says the Astronomy program here is actually legit. You might end up liking it."

I snort, the sound slipping out before I can filter it. "Yeah? Guess I'll have to take her word for it for now."

They grin, but don't tease. That's what gets me. Always has. They know when to joke and when not to. It feels like some kinda magic.

We follow the sidewalk toward the courtyard, passing the bike rack, the patchy lawn, and an interesting statue. I kick at a leftover leaf, watching it skid across the concrete.

"I mean," I add, trying for casual, "astronomical engineering? It's—it was my dream. Building stuff that actually gets into space?"

They laugh, light, warm, and private. "It sounds really awesome."

I shrug. "It is…"

The courtyard opens up ahead of us, quiet except for the fountain's steady rush. A breeze rattles the branches of the big oak tree, scattering a few acorns across the walkway. Everything smells like cut grass and leftover spring rain.

I risk a look at them—just for a second. Their face is soft in the lamplight, eyes narrowed like they're thinking ten things they're not saying. It guts me in the best way.

We reach the fountain and they sit on the edge, elbows braced on their knees. I stay standing for a moment, watching the water catch the light in thin silver ribbons. Then I sit beside them, a careful few inches away.

She exhales, a slow, uncertain breath. "Can I tell you something?" she asks, not meeting my eyes.

My pulse kicks. "Yeah. Always."

"I'm—" she hesitates. "What if this was all for nothing?" Her voice wavers just enough to make my chest tighten.

"What?"

"The competition...what if it was just...time I could've spent getting more than one job? Being useful? What if it won't lead anywhere?"

I shake my head. "Jada...I don't think you wasted anything." The words come out more forcefully than I intend. "You're insanely talented...and people notice your talent all the time. I see it. You can't tell me that means nothing."

She picks at a loose thread on her dress, jaw tightening. "Feels like it might."

"Then let me believe in it for you," I say, softer. "You don't have to carry all of it alone."

She goes still—not frozen, just...listening. Listening in a way that makes something warm flare behind my ribs.

I shift closer, just a fraction, so our knees almost touch. My hand inches toward hers on the stone edge of the fountain. We aren't touching but just near enough that the space between us feels like a live wire.

For one dizzy second, I think she might reach back. Her fingers twitch, brushing the air between us.

But neither of us moves.

We just...hover there.

She looks up at me then, eyes clearer, steadier. "Quite the optimist today, huh?" she laughs, closing herself off again, wiping under her eye. She's quiet for a long beat, staring at the rippling water like she's waiting for it to say something instead of me.

Then, in a small voice that still manages to hit straight through my ribs, he says, "Okay...but what about you? I mean—how are you even going to help me? What *can* you actually do?"

It's not accusatory. It's not impatient.

It's...vulnerable.

Like he's afraid the ground's about to fall out from under his feet and he wants to know if I'll really reach for his hand before he slips. My throat goes dry. Because I don't have a polished plan, or a roadmap, or even a half-baked idea that sounds good out loud.

All I've got is...well nothing, really. Nothing but the truth.

"I have no clue," I admit, laughing once under my breath because the honesty stings and relieves me at the same time. "I don't have a strategy, or a checklist, or whatever we're *supposed* to have by now."

I turn to him then—really look—because he deserves that much.

"But I know I'm not letting you do this alone," I say, softer. "Even if I don't know what comes next, I'll figure it out. I'll do whatever I can. Whatever it takes to keep you here. I mean that."

He goes still beside me.

Not tense, like they're holding their breath around the words I just gave them.

Their hand doesn't move toward mine, but it doesn't move away either, resting on the stone so close I can feel the warmth of it through the cool night air. Almost-touching. Almost something.

They finally exhale, and it sounds like relief braided with disbelief, like no one's ever promised them something like that before. Not without conditions, not without expectations.

And they whisper, "Okay...yeah. Okay."

Just that.

chapter thirty-six

The universe must've known it was competition day, because I woke up with that tight coil in my stomach—the same one I used to get before finals or thunderstorms or anything with even a hint of high stakes.

I'd been planning for a solid week. A week. Me. Planning. Down to the stupid minute.

I had the flowers. Wrapped carefully in craft paper with a tiny yellow ribbon because the florist said it "added charm."

I had the gift: the delicate silver chain with a turquoise crystal. The necklace from the thrift shop.

I had the bus schedule.

I had the rink address saved in my phone, written on my hand, and scribbled on a post-it stuck to my wall.

I wasn't missing this one. Not again.

Not after missing the last one.

Not after how she looked when she talked about the finals.

Not after everything that's happened.

I wasn't losing another person to a date mixup, a stupid mistake, or my own fear.

I wasn't.

So I stood in the hallway, backpack over one shoulder, practically vibrating with nervous energy as I called out:

"Mom? We're leaving in ten!"

Nothing.

"Mom?"

Still nothing.

My chest tightened. I walked to her room, knocked lightly, then louder. Nothing. I walked to the kitchen. Empty. I even checked the hall. Empty. The keys are still here, where could she be?

I pulled out my phone and hit call.

Ring. Ring. Ring.

No answer.

"Come on," I muttered, pacing in tiny frantic circles.

Then finally—*ding.*

Hey baby, I'm at work. What's up?

I froze.

My brain tried to reboot like a glitchy computer.

At work?

At work?

She said she'd be off today. Today was the 13th. She promised. We planned.

I typed with stiff fingers:

Mom, the competition is today! You said you'd be off.

Honey...I'm off on the 14th. She sent back.

My breath stopped dead in my throat. It was like someone took a needle to my lungs and popped them. The bus. She took the bus.

Another date mixup.

Just like last time.

The one that ruined everything.

I tasted metal, like panic was rising into my mouth.

This wasn't happening.

This wasn't happening.

I stared at the message until the letters blurred together, and the edges of my vision tingled the way they did right before a panic attack.

No. No. Not today.

I wasn't letting this happen again.

Before I even realized what I was doing, my body moved on its own.

I grabbed the keys from the hook.

I grabbed my backpack.

I yelled, "Austin! Watch Millie! Don't open the door for anyone!"

Austin blinked at me from the couch, controller in hand, half confused. "Uh—yeah? Sure?"

But I didn't wait.

I couldn't.

My heart was already sprinting ahead of me.

I ran to the elevator, slammed the button, watched the number slowly crawl toward my floor like it was mocking me.

"Nope—nope—nope—" I whispered, and I bolted for the stairs.

Every step felt like it might collapse under me but I took them anyway, two at a time, practically tripping, gripping the rail so hard my knuckles burned.

By the time I burst outside, the cold air slapped me in the face, shocking my system enough to make me realize—

What the hell was I doing?

But my legs were still moving.

Straight to the car.

I yanked the door open, fell into the driver's seat, and the second the door shut, the world shrank into a tiny metal box with no air.

My hands started shaking uncontrollably.

My breath stuttered, quick and sharp and wrong.

The seatbelt felt like a trap.

The steering wheel felt like a threat.

I grabbed the handle above the door like it was the only thing keeping me grounded.

My other hand hovered over the keys, trembling.

I squeezed my eyes shut.

"Okay Payton, breathe. Just breathe. You practiced this. You practiced this with Dr.Flores. You can do this. You can do this. You can—"

My heart didn't believe me.

My lungs definitely didn't.

I could feel the pressure building, like someone was slowly filling my chest with water and waiting to see when I'd drown.

But then I pictured Jada.

Laughing on the ice.

Landing that triple for the first time.

Saying she was scared the competition was a waste.

Asking what I'd do to help her stay.

Me telling her...*promising her* I'd try.

I wasn't going back on that.

Not for fear.

Not for panic.

Not for the ghosts in my head.

My hand, still shaking, found the keys again.

I forced them into the ignition.

Turned.

The engine roared to life and my heart roared with it, terrified and determined at the same time.

I plugged my phone into the aux with a clumsy, shaking motion and scrolled for something loud enough to drown out the noise in my head.

The music hit the speakers hard. Drums, bass, something steady and grounding and I turned it up until the vibrations ran through my ribs.

I took one last breath.

Then another.

Then I whispered, "Don't die. Just...don't die. We can freak out later."

And I pulled out of the parking lot, hands tight on the wheel, heart beating like a warning alarm, driving myself to the rink in the next town over.

To be there for her.

No matter how scared I was.

chapter thirty-seven

I made it with ten minutes to spare.

Barely.

My hands were still shaking when I slammed the car door shut, my body buzzing with leftover adrenaline like I'd swallowed a live wire. Did I even lock the car properly—I think I hit the button? Maybe? But I was already speed-walking toward the rink entrance because if I slowed down, even for a second, my brain was going to realize what I'd just done and shut me down entirely.

Inside was chaos.

Parents holding giant bouquets.

Kids in warm-up jackets stretching in hallways.

Volunteers shouting things like "WRISTBANDS! PLEASE HAVE YOUR WRISTBANDS!"

And me, a single, frantic idiot weaving through the crowd like a salmon with anxiety.

I flashed my entry pass at the checkpoint lady so fast it practically created a breeze. She blinked at me, waved me through, and I muttered a breathless "thankyousorrythankyou" while power-walking deeper into the building.

People stood right in the middle of the walkway as if human traffic didn't exist. I dodged one woman taking a picture, slipped between two teenagers arguing about music, and sidestepped a toddler wielding a french fry like a weapon.

I needed to find Jada.

Now.

My lungs still felt too tight from the drive, the panic clinging to the edges of my ribs, but I pushed forward until I reached the double doors that separated spectators from the competitor area.

And then—there.

They were standing right outside the competitor circle door, bouncing lightly on their skates, warming up their legs. Their jacket hung open, blades glinting under the fluorescent lights. They looked focused, the way they always did before performing. A soft intensity.

"Jada!" I called before I could think.

They turned, and when their eyes landed on me, their whole expression shifted—from confusion to surprise to something warm that made my breath stutter.

"Payton?"

I stopped in front of them, still catching my breath like an asthmatic racehorse.

"Hey," I managed.

They tilted their head, eyes narrowing slightly. "You okay? You look like you ran a marathon."

"I kinda did?" I said, rubbing my face. "Just...not on foot."

They blinked.

Then she stepped closer, really looking at me.

Her voice dropped. "How did you get here?"

I stared at the floor for a second, then mumbled, "I drove."

She froze.

"You...what?" she asked, eyebrows shooting up so fast they nearly left her forehead.

"I drove," I repeated, louder this time, though my voice cracked like it was going through puberty all over again. "By myself."

Her hand flew to her mouth. "Payton—"

"I had to be here," I said quickly, before she could scold me or worry or tell me I was insane. "I wasn't missing this one. Not again."

She opened her mouth, emotion flickering over her face so fast I couldn't name it.

But then I remembered the bag slung over my shoulder.

"Oh—uh—here." I scrambled to pull it off, nearly elbowing a passing competitor. "I, uh—got you these."

I handed her the flowers, pink and white and tiny streaks of lavender, and her eyes widened.

"Oh my god, Payton…" she whispered.

"And—uh—this too."

I placed the necklace box into her palm, my hand shaking slightly from the drive, from the nerves, from everything.

She stared at it like it was something delicate and sacred. She held it for just a second before opening it.

"Payton…you remembered—you didn't have to—what—"

"I know," I cut in softly. "I wanted to."

She looked like she was about to say something. Something big, something that sat behind her eyes glowing like a light through stained glass.

But the door behind us cracked open.

A staff member poked his head out. "Group B! You're up for warm-ups!"

He looked right at her, then down to her sticker. "Number 53! Let's go."

He stepped back inside.

She turned toward the door, then back at me, torn in two directions. "I have to—"

"I know."

And then something inside me moved before I told it to.

I reached out and caught his arm, gently, but firmly enough to stop him from walking into the competitor room.

He turned back, eyes wide.

And I pulled him into a hug.

A real one.

A tight one.

The kind you give someone you're terrified of losing.

His breath hitched against my shoulder.

"Good luck," I whispered, voice cracking on the last word.

He didn't move for a second like he was memorizing it.

Then he nodded against me, pulled back with this small, stunned smile, and said, barely above a whisper:

"I'll find you after."

And then he slipped into the competitor circle, the door shutting behind him, leaving me with my racing heart and the faint smell of ice and roses clinging to my clothes.

chapter thirty-eight

I hate this part. The waiting. The way time
turns syrup-thick and refuses to move, the way
my own heartbeat feels like a fist knocking at
the inside of my ribs.

Jada Knight—number 53, the girl I coached,
the girl I failed once, the girl I refuse to fail again—is
somewhere behind those double doors marked
"Competitors Only," and I'm stuck in the echoing cold
of the stands with nothing but the roar of the crowd
and the weight of everything I never say out loud.

They glide onto the ice like a quiet storm
brewing under a silk sky. Number 53 sticker clean on
their shoulder, their costume catching the rink lights in
glittering flecks that make them look like they were
carved out of a comet's tail.

Even from all the way over here, I see the tiny
shake in their hands. The nervous habit where their
thumb circles their palm. The way they're searching
the stands like they can feel me watching.

And God, I wish I could shout loud enough that they'd hear me: "You're here. You made it. You're ready. Go."

But instead I sit, teeth pressed together, breath too shallow, heart too goddamn loud.

Their music starts with a single violin stroke. Sharp, sweet, crystalline. They push off.

Jada moves like gravity never had a claim on them. Their blades carve ribbons into the surface, every turn sharp as a heartbeat, every extension soft enough to make the whole arena hush as if they're afraid to breathe too loud and break the spell.

And the spell is real. I should know.

Every practice. Every frustrated sigh. Every late night where they grouched at me for choosing the wrong warmup playlist. Every fall. Every bruise. Every shimmering moment where I caught a glimpse of the champion they didn't believe they could be.

And now it's here. Now they're here. Number 53. My Jada. The one I ran through traffic lights and heart attacks to see.

They skate through the first combination flawlessly. The crowd murmurs. I swear I could punch the air.

Then she glides backward into the setup for the jump that has eaten her dreams for months, the triple axel. The demon. The mountain. The one she circled around like a wolf too smart to rush in.

Her arms tighten. Her knee bends. Her breath fogs in front of her like a ghost fleeing her lungs.

She leaps—

—and spins.

Three and a half rotations, neat as a promise.

Her blades kiss the ice on the landing.

And she lands it.

She actually freaking lands it.

My hand flies to my mouth so fast I almost smack myself.

She keeps going like she didn't just break open the universe a little.

By the time the routine ends—him holding the final pose, chest heaving, eyes shining—I don't know if I've breathed once in the entire four minutes.

The applause crashes around the rink. Jada bows. He skates off. The other competitors shuffle around. The judges scribble. The audience buzzes.

And we wait.

God, do we wait.

The last skater finishes. Scores flash. More waiting. My leg bounces so fast the seat shakes. My hands can't stay still. I keep picturing every time I've lost someone because I wasn't where I needed to be.

What if being here isn't enough?

Then the announcer steps up to the mic.

The whole rink inhales as one.

"In third place…"

My stomach drops.

The name isn't Jada's.

"…in second we have…"

My heart falls through the floor.

It's still not her.

It's down to one.

One out of twenty.

One out of every sleepless night she spent chasing this dream.

Jada is standing beside the other skaters backstage; I can see just the edge of her shoulder through the crack in the door. She's shaking.

He's trying not to show it. He's holding his breath.

So am I.

"...and in first place..."

Silence.

Actual silence.

Every sound folds inward until all I hear is the pounding inside my own skull, the blood rush, the world narrowing into a single thin string of hope stretched tight enough to snap.

"...Jadalyn Knight, number fifty-three!"

Time doesn't just stop.

It melts.

The world goes soft around the edges, the colors deepening, the lights fracturing into beautiful halos like the rink itself is exhaling after holding its breath with me. Every face in the crowd turns bright, every cheer becomes a warm rush instead of a roar, every moment tilts into something slow and sacred.

For a heartbeat, everything is quiet in the most beautiful way.

Like the universe just unclenched a fist.

And then

Noise slams back in.

Cheers explode.

The crowd rises like a wave.

And Jada—my Jada, my miracle of a human, steps forward onto the ice as the champion.

I bury my face in my hands and laugh, breathless and shaking and terrified and ecstatic, because I have never, not once, not ever been this proud of anyone in my entire life.

And I'm here.

I made it.

I didn't miss this one.

Thank God.

Thank God.

chapter thirty-nine

The second the medal ceremony ends, the world swallows Jada alive.

Cameras flash. Microphones appear out of thin air. Reporters shout questions like they're trying to hit a moving target. I lose sight of them more than once, swallowed in a sea of congratulatory chaos and overly caffeinated journalists.

I hover at the edge of it all, hands shoved in my pockets, adrenaline still fizzing through my veins like I accidentally drank battery acid. I want to run to them, but I also don't want to mess anything up. This moment is theirs, not mine.

But then—they appear.

Jada slips out through the back of the little winner's area, escaping the mob with the stealth of someone who's been professionally dodging people since birth. Their hair is messy where the medal ribbon mussed it, cheeks pink from exertion, eyes glazed in that dazed, high-altitude happiness that comes after doing the impossible.

And the second they see me, their whole face breaks open into this tired, elated, disbelieving smile.

"Payton."

My name sounds different from them. Softer. A little breathless. Like I'm something worth saying gently.

They walk toward me, medal clinking against their chest. I meet them halfway.

Before I can even get words out, she's thrusting the gold medal up toward my face like a kid showing off a lizard they found under a rock.

"Look," she beams. "Look, look, look."

I laugh because I can't help it. God, her joy is contagious. It spills everywhere. She practically vibrates with it.

"It's real," I say, dumbly.

"It *is* real!," she adds, grinning so hard her eyes almost close. "And heavy. And shiny. And I keep checking to make sure I'm not hallucinating."

I reach out, touch it with one finger. I shouldn't, it's hers, not mine, but she grabs my wrist and presses my hand fully against the metal like she wants me to.

My heart does something illegal in my chest.

Then she digs into her jacket and pulls out a sleek white envelope. The seal's already broken, the corner bent from how many times she's clutched it.

"Payton," she says, softer this time, "look."

She hands it to me.

Inside is the check. The prize money.

Enough to cover the next two—no three—years of tuition. Enough to shift her entire future. Enough to make breathing easier for once in her life.

I stare at it.

Then at her.

Then back at the impossible paper in my hands.

"Jada," I whisper, "you did it. You really—"

"No," she cuts in, stepping closer until we're almost chest-to-chest. "We did this."

He is trembling slightly. Mostly from exhaustion, from adrenaline, and from trying very hard not to collapse into a puddle on the floor. His nose is pink from the cold, his eyes bright, his breath still just a little uneven from skating, winning, surviving all of it.

I can't stop staring at him.

"What?" he asks, voice cracking on the word like he hasn't quite caught up to oxygen returning to his lungs.

"You—" I start, but I can't find the right version of the truth. "I'm just...I'm proud of you."

He swallows. Hard.

"That means more than the medal," he murmurs.

Which is insane. And unfair. And way too much.

I step even closer.

I don't mean to.

My body just...does it.

Like gravity finally figured out who I orbit.

He looks up at me with these tired, glowing eyes, the medal gleaming against his chest, the envelope still clutched in one shaking hand, and everything inside me hits a breaking point.

The good kind.

The kind where something old cracks so something new can breathe.

"Jada," I say, voice barely there.

He tilts his head. "Yeah?"

The world softens.

The rink hum fades.

Somewhere, a Zamboni growls to life but even that feels like it's behind glass.

And then—

I lean in and kiss him.

It's gentle at first. The kind of soft, breathy kiss that feels like asking a question you already know the answer to. His lips are cold from the ice, warm from his skin, trembling from everything he's just lived through.

But then he kisses me back.

And oh, *God*.

His free hand rises to my jacket, gripping the fabric like he's anchoring himself, like the medal and the check and the entire universe are secondary to this one moment.

The world tilts.

The cold air disappears.

Everything becomes pulse and warmth and the feeling of someone choosing you back.

When we finally pull apart, we're both breathing too fast.

He laughs—half disbelieving, half euphoric—and presses his forehead to mine.

"Payton," he says, voice wrecked and wonderful, "you're insane."

"I know," I breathe back. "But I'm here, aren't I?"

He smiles, eyes soft, heart open in a way that makes me feel like I'm standing on holy ground.

"Yeah," he whispers. "You are."

And then, quieter, like a secret meant only for me:

"I'm glad you are."

chapter forty

It's been a few weeks since the competition, but every time I meet Jada in the park, I still feel that little jolt—that quiet *holy crap, they're mine* spark that hits me right in the ribs.

They're stretched out on the grass beside me now, hoodie half-zipped, cheeks sun-warm, hair caught in a breeze that keeps flipping a strand over their forehead. I reach over and fix it without thinking, and they pretend not to smile.

We've done this routine a lot lately. Slow afternoons. Park benches. Me sitting cross-legged, them sprawled out with their arm brushing mine. Their braids spread throughout the blanket on the still slightly dewy grass. The kind of comfort where silence isn't scary anymore.

They roll onto their side, propping themselves up on an elbow.

"So," they say, drawing the word out like they've been waiting to ask it all day, "you're basically graduating in a month."

"Yeah," I exhale. "Kinda wild."

"Kinda?" They snort. "Dude, that's huge. You're getting your associate's. That's a big deal."

They pause, tapping their fingers against the grass. "Do you have...an extra ticket? For the ceremony?"

"Yeah," I say, trying not to sound too eager. "Actually—I was hoping you'd come."

Their face brightens in a way that feels like the sun shifted positions just for me.

"I'd love to," they say. "Obviously."

She sits up fully, tucking her legs under herself, knees brushing against mine. She looks a little embarrassed now, like she's nervous about something. Which is weird because she never looks nervous.

"So then," she says, fiddling with the hem of her sleeve. "Are you...doing anything after? Like, celebrating or whatever?"

I swallow, heart fluttering like it's trying very hard not to give something away too early.

Because I've been waiting for the right moment. And apparently this is it.

"Uh—yeah," I say, trying to be casual and failing miserably. "Actually. I...kind of have something. Well, two somethings."

She raises an eyebrow, holding in a laugh. "Somethings?"

Instead of answering, I reach for my backpack, sliding it closer. My fingers feel stupidly shaky as I unzip the front pocket. I pull out the graduation ticket first—just to hand it to her properly—but then I tug out the second paper and a T-shirt.

I lift the T-shirt first, unfolding it just enough for the design to show.

It's the white-and-yellow version, the one I had printed just for her.

The Birdcage logo stretches across the front in bright gold ink, the little stylized wings catching the light like they're mid-flight.

Her eyes widen, a slow smile curling at the edges. "No way...this is the new variant?"

I nod, heat hitting my cheeks. "Yeah. I, um...thought you'd like the lighter colors. And since you got me into the whole band thing, I...wanted you to have one before everyone else."

She runs her thumb over the printed feathers, gentle like it's something precious. "Payton...this is really cool."

My heart does a somersault. I pretend it's normal.

She takes it and puts it into her bag.

Next, I hold out the crisp, folded letter.

With a very familiar header.

Her eyes widen.

"No way," she breathes. "Payton—no way."

I hand it to her. My heart beats somewhere up in my throat as she opens it.

Her hands fly to her mouth. "You—You applied?"

"Yeah," I say, voice softer than I meant. "I'm going to GSA. Next fall."

And saying it out loud feels like breathing after being underwater for way too long.

She launches forward and wraps her arms around me, half knocking me backward in the grass. I laugh because she's squeezing me so tight I might actually lose circulation, but I don't care, not even a little.

"Payton, that's amazing," she says against my shoulder.

"Yeah," I whisper. "And I'm being for real. No take-backs."

She pulls back, eyes still glassy with joy, cheeks flushed with pride in a way that makes something warm settle heavy inside my chest.

"Okay," she says breathlessly. "I have something too."

When he says that, I blink.

He pulls out his phone and scrolls until he finds whatever he's searching for. Then he hands it to me.

On his screen is a program description.

MIT.

Astroengineering Masters Pathway.

Brand new.

Accepting applicants who complete their bachelor's and want to further their studies.

I stare at it for a long moment before looking up at him.

"You...found this?" I ask, barely getting the words out.

He nods, rubbing the back of his neck like he's embarrassed to admit he spent time researching something for me.

"I remembered what you said," he murmurs. "About wanting to try again. Wanting to...I don't know. Build things. Do something with the stars again. I thought—maybe this would give you another shot."

Something hits me in the chest then. Something deep. Something terrifying in a good way.

"Jada," I breathe, "this means I could actually...do it. I could—"

He smiles, soft and hopeful and so damn proud.

"You deserve to try," he says simply. "And now you can."

And that's it. That's all it takes.

The whole future—this long, complicated, terrifying thing—opens up in front of me like someone finally turned the lights on.

For the first time in years, I don't feel stuck.

Or scared.

Or behind everyone else.

I feel...ready.

Not because the path is easy.

But because I'm not walking it alone.

We sit there for a while—his hand slipping into mine, fingers weaving together like they were always meant to. The wind rustles the trees above us, kids laugh on the swings in the distance, and somewhere a dog barks at absolutely nothing.

And I let myself breathe. Not the panicked kind or the shallow kind. Just...breathe. The future is big. Huge. Blinding sometimes.

But right now?

Right now the world feels manageable. Right now, I feel like I can do it.

Right now, I feel like maybe I'm allowed to be happy.

"Hey," he says eventually, nudging my shoulder with his. "You okay?"

I turn toward him, thumb brushing along the back of his hand, and something in me pulls loose, a gentle, hopeful warmth that's been building ever since the rink, the dance, the competition, all of it.

"Yeah," I say. "Never been better."

He looks relieved in that soft way he gets, where his whole face relaxes and his shoulders drop like he's been holding his breath for me. And before I can second-guess it, I lean in.

He meets me halfway.

It's quieter than the first kiss, with less adrenaline, more gravity. Slower. Certain. The kind of kiss that says we survived the hard parts...and we're choosing the next ones together.

When we break apart, he laughs under his breath, forehead resting against mine.

"What?" I ask, brushing my thumb along his cheekbone.

"You," he murmurs, closing his eyes like he's memorizing the moment. "You look...happy."

I smile. It's real, unforced, steady.

"Yeah," I whisper. "Wonder why."

He rolls his eyes but he's smiling too, and he squeezes my hand again as we sit there in the grass, letting the world settle around us.

And I swear it feels like the universe smiles
back.

authors note

Grief manifests itself in many ways and I
wanted to show that with Payton. I had read
books about grief before, but few fully
resonated with me.

I began writing *When the Ice Breaks* as a junior
in high school. At the time, it was a story about how
unforgiving high school can be. I wanted to feel seen.
High school was brutal for me, especially when that
pain spilled into the theater—the one place I felt safe.
During those years, before my anxiety and depression
were diagnosed, books became my escape. *I Was Born
For This* and *Solitaire* by Alice Oseman were places I
could breathe when everything else felt too loud.

That pain first became Jada, the original main
character, and she remained the heart of the story until
my freshman year of college. That was when Payton
stepped in. His voice felt more natural, more alive, and
more honest. I reshaped the story around him, but it
still wasn't one I was proud of...so I changed things up
a bit.

Like Payton, I lost someone *very* close to me in my freshman year of college. I lost my wonderful grandmother, my Mamma, Nina. She was kind, beautiful, *incredibly* stubborn (me too, my friends and family can attest), and most of all, one of my biggest supporters. She's the reason I still write.

Losing her really solidified what this book was going to be about.

My freshman year of college was also when I began therapy. I was at a very low point, feeling emotions I didn't yet have words for. I was diagnosed with severe anxiety and depression—things I had lived with for years without understanding. Suddenly, everything made sense. Payton became my way to express all of it.

Through him, I poured out what I was feeling and found pieces of myself along the way. This book became about grief, healing, and the quiet hope of knowing you're not alone.

I hope *When the Ice Breaks* can be an escape for someone else, the way those books were for me—and that anyone who sees themselves in Payton knows they are not alone.

acknowledgments

This book has taken so incredibly long to finish. I mean, most books are. But it's crazy to look back and see how much has changed since I started. I was seventeen and I like to think I've changed and gotten better since then.

There are also things that haven't changed. Like the people who've supported me along the way.

Starting off with the two most important people in my life, my mama and padre. Jonnin and Vinny, who've always supported me no matter what I did, whether it be sports, theater, or this. I might've given up if it weren't for them.

My grandma, my mamma, Nina Andersen. Who always wanted to read my writing but I was too scared to show it. Who continued to support me and brag about me to people who had no clue who I was. The woman who told everyone that I was writing a book and it was going to be amazing. The woman who promised to buy every copy. I'll have one for you and it'll be signed just like you wanted when I see you again.

My brother, Andy, who inspired the entire character of Austin and listened to me go on and on about my characters and told me, "slay queen that's awesome." (My favorite straight boy, everyone.)

My best friend, Toby Logan. Who was my rock through the worst years of my life. The boy who inspired Payton as a character. The one who I'd joke about not making it out of high school with, but getting passing grades anyways. The guy who I wouldn't have made it through high school without. Who followed me to the same college. Who I never wanna do life without. (You can't get rid of me, and I can't get rid of you. We know too much about each other for that to happen.) I hope you love this book more than anyone else.

My first ever true friends outside of high school—Christan, Andrew, Jess, Allie, and Alicia. Thank you for never judging me but still calling me out when I do something stupid. Putting up with my stubbornness. Being with me in my toughest moments and supporting me though the past two years. I couldn't have continued to push myself to do this and everything else I've accomplished if it weren't for you. I love you guys.

Sab Ay. I LOVE YOU! Thank you for letting me send you voice note after voice note of rambles about this book and the others to come. I love bouncing ideas around and you telling me they're good and vice versa. You're one of my favorite people to talk to. And I'm sorry for pestering you with all the publishing questions, you're literally amazing. (And the cover!!! I absolutely adore it!!! Thank you so, so, SO much!!!)

CaL, the one who supported, edited, and helped me write nearly an entire scene so it was accurate. Thank you. You always "pestering" me about wanting to read it before it was done made me keep wanting to write because there was always someone who wanted to read it. I'm glad that someone was you. I love you!!

All my online friends—CaL (hi again), Kenzie, Kramic, Lair, Lee, Lilli, Soph, Shock, Syren, and Toni. Thanks for listening to my rambles of a YA Contemporary book set in the real world while most of you write fantasy and two of you write music. And then Moony and Joy, my little sisters from other misters, I love you both. Thanks for offsetting my reality with y'alls super awesome fantasy. I can't wait to read all of your books.

My beta readers—Toni, Lair, Kai Reyes, Gillian Cathcart, Lola, Anna, Heloísa, and CaL (last time I swear lol). Your comments and love for this book made me so unbelievably happy. Thank you for being the first people I shared this book with.

And my followers, commenters, and loyal story likers on Instagram. I hope this story was everything you expected it to be and more.

I love y'all,

K.J.

www.ingramcontent.com/pod-product-compliance
Lightning Source LLC
Chambersburg PA
CBHW070848160726

48004CB00003B/970